RAINFOREST RETREAT

GETAWAY BAY® RESORT ROMANCE, BOOK 7

ELANA JOHNSON

ONE

THE WIND PICKED up as Maizee Phelps came up over the rise of the hill, the beautiful Umauma Waterfall spreading out before her. With her breathing coming quickly, Maizee felt a rush of accomplishment.

She liked nothing better than being outside, among the trees and foliage of Hawaii, the wide, blue sky above her.

Except today, the weather wasn't exactly friendly. With Tropical Storm Eric on the horizon, Maizee supposed she should've been at her new apartment, making sure she had enough groceries for the next few days, and hunkering down.

But she'd just arrived in Getaway Bay three days ago, and she didn't want to spend her weekend before starting at the bank indoors. No, if she could, she'd be out in a kayak, exploring this island she'd only visited as a tourist in the past.

Her calves tightened, but she kept walking until she

found the perfect sketching spot. To her left, she could see the falls, and to her right, the horizon showed the edge of the island and then the gorgeous Pacific Ocean. And way out where the sea kissed the sky, the darkness indicated Eric was indeed alive and well.

The storm wasn't set to hit the island for another day, at least, and Maizee wasn't worried. As a Hawaii native from the island of Lanai, she'd weathered plenty of storms. Too bad she wasn't as good at surviving the relationship disasters in her life.

She sighed as she swung the backpack off her shoulders and set it at her feet. "And you thought Winn was the one." She shook her head, wishing she was brave enough to stay at the same branch as him, face him everyday, and just carry on with her life.

Maybe find someone new, fall madly in love, and show him that he hadn't affected her all that much.

Unfortunately, he had become her whole world over the past five years—one of which where she wore his diamond ring—and she didn't have the stomach to see him each day at work and not go home with him at night.

At least he'd broken things off before she'd booked a wedding venue. She did, however, have a white gown that she now had no use for. She'd asked her mother if she could store it in her childhood closet, and that was where it cuurently hung.

Maizee figured she'd try to sell it one day, perhaps when the memories containing Winn didn't make her chest pinch and her whole countenance sad.

She unzipped her pack and pulled out her sketchpad

before tipping her chin toward the sky. She rolled her shoulders and took a long drink of water from her bottle, moving through her muscles as they started to cool.

Once she had relaxed, she reached back into her pack and found the box of black crayons she took everywhere with her.

She didn't care that Winn had labeled her art "colorless" and "kind of weird." Maizee loved the way crayon could be sharp and thin, or thick, jagged lines, with no defined edges. She felt like the black crayon, sometimes with every piece of jewelry and strand of hair in the exact right place, and sometimes with her hair in a messy bun and more pizza sauce on her T-shirt and fingers than on the actual pie.

"Sit down, Roger," she told her little dog, and the long-haired Jack Russell terrier complied, his tongue hanging out of his mouth. She poured him a bit of water into a collapsible bowl, and the dog lapped at it without standing up.

Maizee drained the rest of the water bottle, hoping she'd make it back to the trailhead before she had to use the restroom, and set the sketchpad on her knees. She always started with the sharpest crayons, and she roughed in the falls, the trees, and the horizon beyond them before switching to a duller one to add in the softer parts of the picture.

She realized how whippy the wind had become when she shivered, the sweat on her neck and forehead chilly now. Glancing up, she found the sky darkening, clouds rolling in from the black spot on the horizon.

Startled, Maizee dropped the crayon she'd been using to add in the finer details. Her heart thumped a bit painfully in her chest. This storm had blown in quickly, and she hadn't even seen it coming.

It certainly wasn't Eric, but she still didn't want to be on this unfamiliar trail in the dark or the rain. She took a few precious seconds to make sure she had everything she'd brought, including every last crayon shaving. Then she shouldered her pack and clipped Roger to the carabiner on her strap, saying, "Let's go, boy."

She cast one last look at the falls she'd been drawing before starting down the path she'd come up. It was only a mile and a half, but she hadn't been in a hurry on the way up. She was now, and the stormclouds continued to steal the light from the day with every step she took.

She estimated she was about halfway down when the first drops of rain splashed against her face. Pausing, she swung her backpack off and dug around inside it for the emergency poncho she never left home without. It was clear, but it would keep her dry, and Maizee knew better than most that it was astronomically better to be dry than it was to be wet. Especially with the wind as strong as it was.

"Come on," she said to the little dog, using him to keep herself centered. She couldn't panic, as that had never helped, and she needed a cool head if she was going to make it back to her car in one piece.

"It's just a little rain, Roger. We'll be okay." But she wasn't comforted by the little rivulets of mud racing down the side of the path with her. She kept to the rockier parts of the trail, thinking the stones would give her the traction she needed as the rain really started to drive down now.

Maizee could barely see in front of her, but she didn't

want to slow down. Gravity seemed to pull on her, helping her get down the trail to the parking lot. She felt near panic, but she just kept moving.

One more step, she thought, her breath sticking somewhere inside her chest. Over and over, she thought it. Kept breathing. She may have offered up a prayer.

And then her one more step went awry, and her ankle twisted painfully. She yelped, threw her arms out in front of her as if there would be something for her to grab onto, and realized she was going down.

She landed on the ground on her hands and knees and quickly rolled onto her backside. The rain made such a ruckus against the plastic poncho, and Roger yowled too.

"Roger," she said, barely able to see the dog. He limped over to her, and a sense of helplessness that felt bottomless filled her. She cradled the little dog while she tried to catch her breath.

Once she did, she tried to look at her ankle, but everything was coated in mud. Pain thrummed through her foot and leg with every beat of her heart, and she had no idea what to do.

"Get up," she told herself through gritted teeth. "You can't lie here in the mud and wait for someone to find you."

There was no one to find her. She hadn't passed a single person going up or down to the falls, and while Maizee had felt utterly alone before, this was a whole new level of isolation. Tears sprang to her eyes, but she refused to let them out. Crying never helped anything. It didn't get her job back. Didn't help get her boyfriend back. Didn't make her boss do much of anything but transfer her to a new branch on a different island in the hopes that "a fresh start" would be what she needed.

But right now, she needed the rain to stop and the sun to come back out. She needed a warm bath and then a warmer blanket.

Roger barked, a high-pitched yelp that Maizee imagined meant, "Help!" in canine. He squirmed away from her and trotted away until the leash tightened. He barked again, facing down the path instead of up toward the falls the way Maizee was.

"I can get up," she told him, but he continued to yap like his life depended on it. Maizee braced both hands against the slick mud and pushed herself over onto her knees. Now, she just needed to get her feet under her, and she'd get back to her car and assess the damage from there.

Balanced on her hands and knees, she put her weight on her good foot, and pushed. As pressure came down on her injured ankle, it buckled again. She cried out, which sent Roger into a tizzy, and sank back to the earth.

She let a few tears out now, mostly because of the white-hot pain in her foot, but also because she couldn't see an acceptable way out of this dilemma. No one even knew where she was. No one in her neighborhood even knew her name. She'd spent the three days she'd been on this island getting her house set up and filling it with food and basic home goods.

Her new job started on Monday, and she'd been looking forward to a relaxing weekend before her real life had to start again.

No one would see the tears among the rain anyway. There wasn't anyone to see anything.

And yet, Roger barked like he was sending a message to someone, somewhere. Maizee tried to shush him, but he would not be silenced. So she ignored him while she took off her pack and started rummaging around inside. Maybe she could make something that would support her ankle enough to get her off this trail.

She took a couple of painkillers, and the simple nature of the action calmed her a little. Taking a deep breath, she pulled out her first aid kit, wishing she'd had the foresight to put a brace inside. But all she had were Bandaids, moleskin, gauze and medical tape, and hand sanitizer. She had the sketchpad and the crayons, as well as a length of rope, a pair of nail clippers, and a bag of the peppermint mints she liked to suck on while she hiked.

And a tall Gatorade bottle.

She pulled it out and grabbed the medical tape. She couldn't fit the bottle down into her shoe, but she turned it upside down so the narrower end was at her heel and she taped the bottle to her ankle and leg, the pressure painful until she moved up higher on her calf.

"All right," she said, once again praying her makeshift brace would help. She zipped everything back inside her pack and tried to stand again. She got to her feet this time, but stood on the path, the toe on her injured foot barely touching the ground as she balanced on her other foot.

She didn't see how she could take a step on her injured leg, Gatorade bottle or not. She took a deep breath and prepared herself to fall again when she heard a distinct voice calling through the rain.

"Hello? Is anyone there?"

"I'm here," she yelled, her voice more shrill than she liked. But at this point, she couldn't care. "Up here. I'm up here!"

A figure came through the rain, becoming more and more defined with every step up the trail he took.

He was a tall man, wearing a hooded jacket and a pair of jeans. At least he wore a decent pair of shoes as he came closer and closer.

"I did hear a dog," he said as Roger jumped up on him, marring his pants with mud. Maizee should've corrected her animal, but she honestly couldn't look away from the man who'd miraculously showed up to save her.

She knew him. Lawrence Gladstone—the owner of the bank where she'd worked for the past nineteen years.

No, they had never met in person—she would've remembered that. But everyone who worked at Gladstone Financial knew who Lawrence was.

"Are you okay?" His dark, dreamy eyes ran from her foot to her face and back again. "You have a bottle taped to your leg." He had to shout to be heard over the rain, but that only ensured that Maizee could hear the bass quality of his voice.

"I fell down," she said, wondering why he could look like male perfection in a rainstorm while she surely looked like a drowned rat. "Twisted my ankle."

"Can you walk?"

"I don't think so. I just barely managed to get up." She

tugged on Roger's leash to get him to settle down, but the dog seemed as anxious to get off this trail as Maizee was.

"Well, let's see what we can do." He stepped to her side, and she admired the neat beard and mustache he wore. "I'm going to put my arm around you." He did, and she lifted hers over his shoulders with a groan.

"Okay, let's try." He stepped and she tried, but her ankle was not accepting any weight and she almost pulled them both to the ground.

Lawrence grunted and steadied her before taking a step back. "All right, so that's out." He glanced around. "We better find somewhere to ride out this storm. Then I can make a call."

Of course he could. She was surprised he hadn't already, that the Coast Guard, all the officers at the naval base on the island, and every local cop, paramedic, and firefighter weren't already on their way here.

Instead of saying anything, she just nodded as if she knew a good spot where they could ride out the storm. But she didn't.

TWO

LAWRENCE GLADSTONE HATED THE OUTDOORS, and all this rain and mud were exactly why. Who in their right mind went hiking? Apparently this woman standing beside him, all of her weight on her left leg.

Under drier conditions, he could probably carry her down the trail and get her on her way home. But in this downpour, he could barely see two feet in front of his face, and everything felt like it had been rubbed down with coconut oil.

He ran his hand through his hair, wishing it wasn't quite so full of water, and readjusted his hood in an attempt to keep the rain out.

Of course, the one time he'd decided to see what outdoor recreation this island had to offer, it had turned into a natural disaster.

"I think we should just try to get down," the woman said, drawing Lawrence's attention back to her. She looked like she'd been out in the rain for a while, but some parts of her were still dry because of the poncho she wore. She also had a backpack, which made the score her: 2 and him: 0.

He'd thought he'd just take a little stroll up to a waterfall. Then he'd be able to tell his friends at the Nine-0 Club that he'd left the house. Maybe take a selfie with the falls in the background and post on social media that he did go outside from time to time.

He wasn't sure why people did that, when there were movies and the Internet inside, but even he had to admit he was looking a little pale this summer. But he was comfortable behind a screen or reading a financial report, and he honestly saw no reason why he needed to relax just because he lived on a tropical island.

"I don't think you can walk," he said. "And we're about another quarter of a mile to the parking lot."

"That's two blocks," she said, and something about her was familiar. She had blonde hair and blue eyes, with the kind of tall, lithe frame Lawrence usually liked. "I can go two blocks." She wore determination in those eyes, and her jaw clenched.

There was something about her that made his blood run a little hotter, and in this rain, he welcomed the warmth.

"All right." He put his arm around her again, his pulse pounding for a few reasons. One, he was legitimately worried she'd pull him to the ground. And two, underneath the mud and rain, she smelled like flowers.

She gripped his jacket on the far shoulder, pressing the length of her body against his. "All right," she repeated. "You step, and I'll go with you."

Lawrence just wanted to find a tree they could hide under for a while. But he employed his bravery—something he'd been trying to do more and more lately—and stepped with his far leg. Next step, she'd have to put weight on her injured ankle—or him.

They did it, moving only a few inches forward. But it was something. And they stepped again and then again, Lawrence's breath laboring through his lungs. He wasn't carrying her, but it felt like he was, and as the ground leveled, he caught sight of a huge banyan tree that could offer some protection.

"Over here," he said, steering her in the direction of the tree. She didn't protest, and by the time they arrived under the leaves and branches of the banyan, he was out of breath —and so was she.

She sank to the ground, which was much drier here and said, "Thank you," through her panting. She un-taped the bottle and let it roll away. Her eyes closed, and she lay down on the ground, crossing her arms over her chest.

Alarm sang through Lawrence. Maybe she was going into shock. Maybe he shouldn't let her rest like this. He honestly had no clue. Born and raised in New York City, his definition of the outdoors was the boardwalk at Coney Island. Or a walk through Central Park.

"What's your name?" he asked, hoping that would keep her awake and get her talking.

"Maizee Phelps," she said, her breathing starting to even out. He still felt like he'd swallowed a lungful of seawater, so she was definitely in better shape than him.

"Maizee Phelps," he said. "And what do you do here on the island?"

"I'm starting a new job on Monday." Her blue eyes opened and she looked at him. Lightning could've struck the banyan, and Lawrence wouldn't have known it. He couldn't look away from her, and time seemed to slow. The pounding rain muted, and it wasn't until her dog crawled onto her stomach, crinkling the plastic poncho, that Lawrence realized he'd fallen into a trance.

He shook himself, pushed his hood off, and ran both hands through his wet hair. "That's great," he said, feeling out of sorts. At least he'd told Linus, his next-door neighbor, where he was going this afternoon. That way, someone would know where to come look for his body.

Stop it, he told himself. This was a little rain. Some wind. He wasn't going to die today. It only felt like it.

"Where will you be working?" he asked, hoping it was somewhere he might be able to drop by and see her from time to time. Maybe Monday. And then Tuesday.

"Gladstone Financial?" She put a question mark on the end of it, as if he wouldn't know the institution.

His breath stuck in his chest, and all the heat that had entered his blood rushed out. "Oh," he said, all fantasies of stopping by Maizee's place of employment until he was brave enough to ask her out dying on the spot.

He'd see her on Monday all right, because he owned Gladstone Financial and had a huge corner office in the branch he'd established here in Getaway Bay.

"I'm Lawrence Gladstone," he said, thinking he might as well get the introduction out of the way. His heart wailed. He'd never disliked who he was until that moment, until it meant he couldn't ask for Maizee's number and fall asleep with the image of her pretty face in his mind.

He did not date employees. Period. The end. It had never ended well that he could tell, and he thought this was one area where he didn't have to have personal experience to know an office romance was a bad idea.

"I know," she said. "I've worked for Gladstone Financial for nineteen years."

"Ah." Lawrence nodded and looked away, a definite measure of unhappiness pulling through him. Of course, the one woman who had made his pulse accelerate in the past decade had to work for him.

Of-freaking-course.

The tension between them was palpable now, and this situation was almost as bad as the hiking had been.

———

"I'm never going hiking again," he said to his empty penthouse, pulling his clothes off as he walked further down the hall and into the kitchen. Standing just in his boxers—which were also soaking wet—he pulled three cans of Dr. Pepper out of the fridge.

He popped the top on one of them and downed almost the whole thing. Since he'd given up drinking so he could always have his best mind present, he'd found flavored sodas and fallen in love. He poured the other two cans over ice in the biggest cup he owned and pulled down the coconut and cherry syrups he kept in the cupboard next to the fridge.

With two pumps of cherry and one of coconut, his dirty Dr. Pepper would be delicious. And he'd let it marinate while he warmed up in the shower.

He didn't employ a maid, though he could certainly afford one. So he swept his disgusting clothes off the floor and stuck them in the washing machine. He used a quick mop to get the floors clean, and then he finally moved into the marble bathroom to get warm.

With his face in the spray, he closed his eyes and finally breathed enough relaxation into his body. Maizee's face formed in his mind, and that only put him in a more terrible mood.

So he hadn't had a date in while. He normally didn't mind, because he had friends and work to keep him occupied. After all, Lawrence could look through financial documents for hours just for fun.

He had his Nine-0 Club meetings, and he really enjoyed spending time with the other billionaires in Getaway Bay. Nina and Jewel Captaine had joined recently, and he'd thought maybe he could capture one of their eyes.

But they both had boyfriends and didn't live on the island permanently anyway. They could, should they choose to do so, but apparently their life in Los Angeles was just as exciting as this tropical paradise.

Lawrence didn't see how, but then again, he'd just started exploring this island where he'd lived for the past five years. He'd always known it was beautiful; he just didn't realize how his surroundings could influence him as strongly as they did.

He finished showering and returned to the kitchen for his drink. His streaming service would keep him company for the night, and he could ignore any texts from Ira or Fisher about how the hike had gone.

Before he could take his drink and become besties with his couch, someone knocked on his door. As one of three penthouse residents in this beautiful building on the southern tip of the East Bay, Lawrence knew only two other people would even have access to this floor.

So he didn't check through the peephole before opening the door to find Linus and his wife, Isabella, standing there. "Hello, Dawseys," he said easily, leaning into the doorway with a smile forming on his face.

The elderly man also smiled. "Just checking to see if you'd made it back." He tossed a glance over his shoulder. "It turned nasty out there."

Isabella reached up and brushed a long piece of his hair back. "You look tired, Lawrence," she said, and his heart squeezed. She reminded him so much of his own grand-mother, and he loved his next-door neighbors.

"I'm going to get him some cell salts," Isabella said, unlatching her arm from Linus's. "Won't take but two minutes."

"We can't be late," he called after her as she went down the hall toward their place. "We have a charity dinner tonight."

"Mm." Lawrence looked at Linus again. He'd had Fisher look into the Dawseys, and while they had quite a lot of money, it wasn't in the billions, and therefore, they didn't qualify for the Nine-0 Club. "Which charity?"

"It's for the new football team," Linus said, and Lawrence remembered all the Sunday afternoon and Monday night invitations over to the Dawsey's penthouse to eat and watch the games. Apparently, Linus was a huge fan, and Isabella loved making tailgating treats.

Lawrence was not opposed to spending a few hours with the Dawsey's, and he liked to eat as much as the next man, especially if the food was good.

"Oh, right," Lawrence said. "Do they start this season?"

"Next fall," he said. "If they can get enough funding and support. They've got a site for the stadium, and apparently a coach and a manager." Linus came alive when talking about football, and Lawrence appreciated that he had something he was passionate about.

Unfortunately for Lawrence, that was usually tax laws and return on investment percentages. And no one wanted to talk with him about those things for longer than a few seconds. Well, maybe Jasper and Ira. Maybe.

"That's great," Lawrence said as Isabella returned. Her gray hair had been swept up onto the top of her head, and she wore a ball gown. So this must be a fancy charity dinner, with plates that cost in the hundreds.

"Here you go," she said, handing him a package of small, white pills. "Straight in your mouth. Take a drink if you want to dissolve them faster. You should feel better in about thirty minutes."

How she knew he felt discouraged and depleted just by looking at him, Lawrence wasn't sure. "Thank you," he said.

"And hey, let me know if they need more donations. I could write a check."

"Great." Linus smiled a final time and then guided Isabella over to the elevator.

Lawrence took the cell salts as instructed, definitely washing them down with several gulps of his soda, and collapsed onto the couch.

His phone chimed, and for half a second, he thought it might be Maizee, thanking him for staying with her until the rain subsided. Then helping her down the mountain to her car. And following her to the hospital in Getaway Bay. He'd stayed beside her on the chair too, trying to figure out if he could ask for her number without coming off as creepy.

So yes, he was considering breaking his dating rules.

She seemed worth it, and while they hadn't spoken a whole lot while they waited for someone to take her back into the ER, he definitely felt comfortable with her. She'd sparked something in him that had been dormant for so long, Lawrence wasn't even sure what it was.

But the text wasn't from Maizee, because Lawrence had not conjured up the courage he needed to ask her for her number.

Which meant it was one of his billionaire friends, none of whom he wanted to talk to at the moment.

THREE

MAIZEE STOOD in front of the mirror, making a tiny adjustment to her earring. She told herself she'd be this meticulous about her appearance for her first day on any job, and that Lawrence Gladstone had no influence over her.

So maybe she was lying to herself.

She'd been reading articles written by Lawrence for years, as Gladstone Financial sent out a monthly newsletter for all of its employees. She knew he was smart and so good-looking it was almost a crime.

But meeting him in the flesh was completely different than seeing a small picture of him on her computer screen. She'd been instantly attracted to him, and he'd shown her kindness for hours, even staying with her at the hospital until a nurse took her back into one of the emergency curtains.

Thankfully, her ankle had not been broken. Just a bad sprain, and she'd been elevating it and putting ice on it to keep the swelling down. She took more ibuprofen than was probably safe, but she would not be missing her first day at work.

She couldn't wear the heels she normally would, but she told herself it didn't matter. She probably wouldn't see Lawrence anyway.

"You don't care if you do see Lawrence," she told her reflection. "And be sure to call him Mister Gladstone." She smoothed down an errant strand of her blonde hair and appreciated the perfect wings she'd gotten on her eyeliner that morning.

"This is going to be a good day." She took a big breath and smiled at herself before turning to leave.

Twenty minutes later, she entered the bank with a key she'd gotten from the branch manager—a man by the name of Willie McMahon.

Because it was only eight o'clock, she knew she'd be the first one in the bank. But she didn't care. She knew where her office was, and she wanted to put a potted plant on her desk. She usually put up pictures too, but she hadn't brought them in today for some reason. Maybe she didn't want to make this new office in this new branch on this new island to be permanent. Not with her parents still living on the island of Lanai, with both of her sisters very nearby them.

Maizee was gone now, and while she wanted her family to be surrounding her in this new place, she thought seeing them might sting too much. At least for today.

She turned on her computer and sifted through the software on it. Maizee should be counting her blessings that there was a branch so close to her beloved Lanai that needed a senior loan officer. Otherwise, she might find herself sitting by herself in a bank in Arizona or Arkansas.

Maizee pushed away her melancholy mood. This was her chance at a fresh start, and she wasn't going to dwell on Winn anymore. After all, Winthrop Porter had already taken too many years of her life from her. Years she'd never get back. He didn't deserve another day.

So she breathed in again, took a sip of her coffee, and opened her email using the username and password she'd gotten from the IT guy at the branch. At least Lawrence made sure his employees were taken care of.

Slowly, as the hour passed, the bank around her became busier as more people arrived at work. She'd met them all a couple of weeks ago when she'd been offered the job, but it would take her some time to remember all of their names.

The coffee dictated when she got up from her desk, her need to use the restroom driving her, and she'd just stepped through the doorway and into the main part of the bank when Lawrence pushed through the glass doors straight ahead of her.

She gasped, freezing at the glorious sight of him in a two-thousand dollar suit, his dark-roast coffee-colored hair swept to the side like a movie star. He pulled sunglasses from his face and kept his focus on his phone at the same time.

He tucked one arm of his glasses in his jacket pocket, his thumbs flying as he typed out a message to someone. Maizee desperately wished her phone would chime when he hit send, but he'd never asked for her number.

She'd thought about asking for his, but she hadn't been

able to come up with a reason why she needed it. And the last thing she needed was to come off as desperate. Besides, she wasn't going to date someone at work again, and Lawrence was like the Top Dog. The owner of the whole company, not just some manager.

No way. She could admire him from afar and hate everyone he went out with just fine.

He navigated the space without looking up—until the staircase only a few steps from her office door. Of course, his office would be on the second floor, but Maizee watched as he misjudged the steps because his phone had completely consumed his attention.

He stumbled and threw his hand out to catch himself on the handrail, but it wasn't enough. He fell, his phone making a loud cracking noise on the hard steps.

"Lawrence," she said, realizing she'd already used the wrong name a moment too late. She reached him in only a second, and he cradled his face. Didn't matter. Blood appeared between his fingers, and Maizee put her hand under his arm. "Come on. I have tissues in my office."

He came with her, and she tried to use her body to shield him from the rest of the bank as she moved him into her office. "Sit here."

He complied, collapsing into the chair across from her desk. She ripped a half-dozen tissues from the box and handed them to him. "Lean your head back."

He did that too, took the tissues, and pressed them to his face. His eyes met hers, and that same electric shock that had jumpstarted her heart underneath that banyan tree struck again.

Maizee did not let herself slip too far into those dark eyes. She cleared her throat and hurried around to the other side of her desk. "I have some painkillers too." She'd need them for her ankle later today.

He shook his head. "I'm fine," he said, his voice muffled by the tissues. "How's your ankle?"

"It's okay," she said. "Not broken, just sprained. I'm wearing a brace for a while." A flush crept into her face, and she really wished it wouldn't. She also didn't know how to make it go away. Her coffee was gone, so she couldn't hide behind the to-go cup, and the hot liquid wouldn't have done anything to cool her down anyway.

"I was going to call you," he said, wiping his nose with the tissues and glancing at them.

Maizee stood up and offered him her garbage can, where he tossed the used tissues before taking more. "You were? Why?"

"Just to make sure you were okay," he said. "But then I realized I never got your number."

Maizee had no idea what to say. Was he asking for her number now? Her heart jumped around inside her chest, almost painfully. She had no idea what she was doing. Her break-up with Winn was only a couple of months old, and she was nowhere near ready to start dating again.

Was she?

"I'm okay," she finally managed to say. She took her seat behind her desk again, using it as a physical barrier between the two of them.

"Well, at least you've seen me bloody now," he said with a chuckle, wiping his nose one more time. The bleeding seemed to have stopped. "So maybe we're even?" He lifted his thick eyebrows, and Maizee almost swooned.

"I think me being mud-covered and unable to walk is worse than a little bloody nose," she said, smiling despite her brain's direct instructions not to do so. Her body seemed to be acting of its own accord no matter what her mind was saying.

Lawrence laughed again, a delectable sound Maizee wanted to hear right in her ear just before he kissed her.

Her whole body felt like someone had placed it over a fire, and she needed to get out of this office immediately. She stood, her chair flying out and hitting the wall behind her. "I have to get some files," she said, when really she'd be running to the bathroom—and not just to hide. "Excuse me."

"Of course." Lawrence stood too, but she didn't wait for him to leave. She rushed past him, still getting a noseful of his spicy and soft cologne. He smelled like the beach and the forest at the same time, which was completely unfair.

Maizee made it to the bathroom and locked herself in a stall, her heart galloping like a herd of wild horses. "Calm down," she whispered to herself. "He's your boss."

Boss, boss, boss.

He was so much more than that, and Maizee knew it.

She stayed in the bathroom for much longer than she needed to, but it took a while for her to strengthen her resolve to keep things with everyone at work in the professional category.

Especially Lawrence.

The sun beat down on Maizee as she tried to make her body move into the position the beach yoga instructor seemed to do so effortlessly.

Her shoulder strained, but Maizee enjoyed the pull, the heat, the smell of suntan lotion and sand and sweat.

She'd been coming to the morning yoga classes before heading into the bank all week, and today, a Saturday, she wouldn't have to pretend she didn't see Lawrence when he arrived. Fake like she was busy so he didn't know she watched and noted the moment he left.

Sometimes he left at a normal quitting time. Sometimes he stayed after she'd left. Sometimes he left in the middle of the afternoon and didn't come back, at least not before she went home.

She wished she didn't have such tight tabs on what he did. But hey, she wasn't following him around…yet.

"Feel the energy from Mother Earth," Tawny said, and Maizee focused on her yoga. She didn't need Lawrence to permeate every aspect of her life, though her work relationships were the source of her friendships.

She'd met one neighbor this week, but the man in his late twenties hadn't been terribly friendly. He'd stood on the sidewalk until a woman in a bright yellow convertible pulled up, and he'd gotten in the passenger seat before they'd driven away.

The girl at Roasted, the coffee shop Maizee visited every morning, had invited her to go boating later that afternoon, and Maizee had said yes. She didn't want to spend her weekends cooped up in her house, baking or thinking about baking. Or doing yard work, which was infinitely worse.

Kara had seemed nice, and Maizee had a phone she could use if she felt uncomfortable that evening.

"That's it for this morning," Tawny said, straightening. "Let's cool down."

Maizee went along with the stretches, Tawny's voice soothing and the fact that she glistened with sweat comforting. Maizee clapped along with everyone else when the class ended, and she reached for her towel.

She wiped her face, enjoying the Hawaiian sun even though the beaches would be full of tourists within the next hour. She didn't mind so much, but Lanai wasn't nearly as popular as somewhere like Getaway Bay.

Maizee caught sight of two businessmen walking along the wooden beachwalk. She stalled, though surely one of them couldn't be Lawrence. What would she do even if one was? Follow him?

No. She shook her head and continued wiping her neck. She would not become a stalker just because the man had great hair. He'd waved at her a couple of times this week, but it seemed like he'd decided to ignore her the same way she was him.

But she couldn't tear her eyes from the pair of men, and it didn't take long for her to recognize the gait of one Lawrence Gladstone. Maizee took her time leaving the beach yoga area so she could watch him enter the Sweet Breeze Resort and Spa with the other man.

The largest building in Getaway Bay, Sweet Breeze had hundreds and hundreds of rooms. Maizee would never find Lawrence.

Though he can't live there, she thought. He was probably

having lunch or something. Brunch. Late breakfast.

"Whatever," she muttered under her breath. She'd spent entirely too much time on Lawrence this week already. The man clearly wasn't interested in her. He'd helped her in a rain storm, and she'd given him tissues.

The end.

Her phone rang, and she swiped on the call from her youngest sister Juliet. "Hey, Jules."

"May-zee," her sister singsonged, and Maizee braced herself for a squeal or a shriek. After that, jealousy would hit her, and she'd be glad she wasn't in the same room as Juliet so she didn't have to keep her true emotions from showing on her face.

"What's the news?" Maizee asked, her voice bright.

"Johnny asked me to marry him!" The shriek came. As did the jealousy. And Maizee turned her face toward the sun, hoping for some of the golden light and hope to infuse into her so she could be happy for her sister.

But Johnny? What kind of name was that? She'd met the man, and she thought he could've at least started going by John once he hit puberty.

"That's great," Maizee said, forcing a smile to her face so it would come through in her voice. "I'm so happy for you. Tell me about it."

She'd gotten so good at those last four words. Then Juliet would talk for a while, and all Maizee had to do was agree every so often, or ask another question that would set her sister off again.

The door closed behind the tall, broad-shouldered form of Lawrence, and Maizee turned toward the bay while Juliet launched into how Johnny had proposed. The story lasted until Maizee returned home, when Juliet finally said she had to go.

Maizee went inside her house, the silence as annoying as it was comforting. Roger trotted out to meet her, and she bent down to scrub him behind the ears. "Hey, boy. Want to go for a walk today?"

Her ankle had improved each day, and she'd been exercising it at the same time she gave Roger the fresh air he needed.

So she got out his leash and clipped it to his collar, her mind telling her that she liked this simple life. Wanted it. And that a man like Lawrence Gladstone would only complicate everything.

FOUR

LAWRENCE SAT on a lounger beside Fisher DuPont's private pool, his soda glass already empty. He could get up and refill it any time he wanted, but Lawrence wasn't feeling particularly up for doing much more than lying around today.

In fact, sitting beside the pool for a couple of hours this morning would give him more sun than he'd had all week.

So his goals to get out and explore the island of Getaway Bay had sort of stalled. Big deal. No one knew of his personal goals, and he could change them any time he wanted.

His company was fine. Better than fine. Doing great, with a eight percent gain over last quarter so far this summer. September was shaping up to be one of the best months, which would hopefully earn them their highest profits in the history of Gladstone Financial.

Normally, he loved sitting beside Ira and talking business, but today, Ira had his hand securely in Gabi's already, and they had their heads bent together as they spoke in low voices. Lawrence hated whispering, but he adjusted his sunglasses and leaned back in his lounger.

He didn't have to talk just because he'd come to the Nine-0 meeting. Kaelin sometimes just sat there, brooding. Tyler could miss several meetings and then show up as if he hadn't been gone at all.

Nina and Jewel walked onto the pool deck, both wearing swishy, flowing cover-ups and huge sunglasses. Both blondes, Lawrence wished his pulse would increase at the sight of them. They never wore anything he'd ever seen before, because they designed their own clothes for their huge online boutique.

It was amazing to him what became popular, but they'd made over a billion dollars in revenue in the first twelve months of launching wearit.com, with profits doubling that in the two years since.

Their latest venture was beachwear, thus their appearance on the island this past eight months or so. Fisher had welcomed them to the Nine-0 Club within a week of them landing in Getaway Bay, which was fine with Lawrence.

Nina and Jewel typically stuck together, but today they sat beside Gabi and drew her out of her conversation with Ira.

Lawrence was *bored,* but he didn't have anything else to do or anywhere else to be. He let Maizee drift through his mind, and a measure of relaxation moved through him.

He could get her number. Find out where she lived now, and where she'd come from. Surely all of that information was in her file at work, and if not, he could certainly discover it in other ways. He liked to think he could learn anything he wanted about anyone, but he didn't want to search through Maizee's file and then call her.

What would he even say? *Hey, I got your number from the employee directory....*

Yeah, that would go over well with the beautiful, well-dressed, competent loan officer. He sighed, unsure as to why he couldn't simply ask her to dinner. Maybe he would be the exception to the rule. Maybe his workplace romance would work out. Just because he'd never seen one that did didn't mean they all ended in complete failure.

"What's eating you?" Ira asked, and Lawrence bent his head toward his friend.

"Nothing."

Ira laughed, a dry sort of chuckle. "I don't believe that for a second."

Lawrence could talk business with Ira for hours and hours, but he didn't want to discuss a woman who'd been plaguing him since the day he'd seen her lying in the mud on the Umauma Waterfall trail.

"No, really, it's nothing." He scooted to the edge of the lounger. "I just have to go. I'm doing a private tour this afternoon."

Ira shook his head. "I don't know why you do that. You don't need the money."

No, he didn't. "I like getting out on my sailboat," he said. "And taking other people out gives me a reason to do it." Otherwise, he might not go. He wasn't sure why, other than sometimes he wanted to go sailing, but the thought of getting everything ready and actually going wore him out before he'd even started.

So he did charters on the weekends sometimes. Today, he'd booked a small group of friends for a few hours, nothing major.

He signaled to Fisher that he was going, and then he pressed the button to call the elevator. Fisher met him there before the car arrived, and asked, "You okay?"

"Just fine." Lawrence looked at Fisher, the man who'd changed Getaway Bay with his hotel and his secret club. "I've got a charter this afternoon, and I want to check the weather and the whale watching boards."

"Sounds great," Fisher said with a smile. "Stacey wants to learn how to sail."

"You guys should come out on the boat," he said. "Anytime."

"Yeah." Fisher glanced back toward the pool and the other Nine-0 members. "Maybe after the baby is born."

The elevator arrived with a *ding!* but Lawrence didn't get in. In fact, Owen and his wife Gina got off, both dressed for a long afternoon at the pool.

"You're going to have a baby?" Lawrence asked.

Fisher laughed and turned back to the pool. "Now that everyone's here, I have an announcement to make."

Lawrence let the elevator close behind him, deciding he could stay for a few more minutes, that his check on the weather could wait.

"Stacey and I are expecting another baby," Fisher called to everyone at the pool, Stacey herself walking over to him and tucking herself against his side.

A cheer went up, and Lawrence participated too, clapping and whooping along with everyone else. After all, Fisher was one of his best friends, and Lawrence enjoyed sharing their successes and happiness.

Esther and Marshall approached them first, so Lawrence waited to say congratulations. They already had a son who would be turning three by Christmas, and Lawrence watched him splashing in the pool with Esther's daughter, Ella.

He shook hands with Fisher and hugged Stacey and said, "Congrats, you two."

"I didn't mean to keep you," Fisher said. "Go, go. Check on your whales."

Lawrence chuckled, but he did head for the elevator and then his penthouse. His mind circled around the happiness of his friends. So many of them had found someone to share their lives with. They'd started families and made commitments. They had more in their lives than a corner office and a company they ran.

Why couldn't he?

He could. He just hadn't known he wanted that life—until he'd met Maizee.

So he'd ask her for her number on Monday. Simple as that.

———

Lawrence put chilled bottled water in all the cup holders on the front seating area of the boat. He had more in the fridge down below, as well as all the snacks the girls would need.

He'd checked the weather, and while the tropical storm had originally been predicted to get close to the islands, it had turned and gone in another direction days ago.

Not only that, but a pod of three pilot whales had been spotted earlier that day in the area he was planning to sail. The wind was scheduled to stay around long enough for him to use it, and he checked the lines one final time before a woman said, "Hello?"

He dashed over to the other side of the boat and grinned down at the brunette he'd met a few weeks ago when he'd given her a tour of his boat and booked her excursion. "Hey, Nan. Come on up."

"Let me text everyone," she said. "They should be here soon." She climbed the ladder and swung herself onto the boat.

Lawrence shook her hand, still smiling. "Still the six of you?"

"I think there's seven now," she said. "Is that a problem?"

"Not at all." He turned and took a few steps. "Let me just grab another bottle of water." Her excursion could accommodate up to eight people, so one more didn't influence her price or what Lawrence would do.

He went down below and came back up to find more women had arrived and were climbing aboard.

He switched gears and headed over to the ladder so he could offer a hand if they needed it. They each exclaimed over the extravagance of the boat as they arrived. They greeted each other with hugs and smiles, and Lawrence wished one of them would excite him even half as much as

Maizee did. Then maybe he wouldn't have to make a fool of himself at work on Monday.

"Thank you," a woman said, drawing his attention away from the group gathering in the bow.

He turned at the familiar voice to see the beautiful blonde he'd been thinking about. "Maizee?"

"Lawrence?"

His hand around hers tightened, and he didn't want to let go. He also had no idea what to say.

"What are you doing?" She leaned in as she spoke, her voice lowering just a little. "You give sailboat tours on the weekends?"

Foolishness raced through him, and his face heated. "Just for fun," he said, as if that made it better.

"You own the biggest financial company in the world," she said next, and Lawrence brought his free hand to his lips.

"Sh," he said in a near whisper. "They don't know that." In fact, very few people knew that.

"They don't?"

"I like sailing," he said. "But…." He didn't want to say he didn't like going out by himself. That it was much more fun if he had people with him, even if they were strangers. They enjoyed it so much, and he liked that he could provide something for them they couldn't achieve themselves.

"You made it." Another woman stepped beside Lawrence, and Maizee smiled at her.

"I did." She slipped her hand out of Lawrence's—he didn't even realize he was still holding it—and moved away.

He watched her go, completely drunk on the sight, the smell, the feel of her on his boat.

She wore a white sundress that showed her bronze shoulders, and Lawrence felt like he might faint. He cleared his throat, reminding himself that he was the man in charge of the largest financial company in the world.

So he liked to sail too. Big deal.

He could still captain this boat—and maybe, if he could be brave enough, he could end this night with Maizee's number in his phone.

"All right, ladies," he said, stepping over to the bow. "Let's go over a few rules, and then we'll get out on the ocean."

He met Maizee's eye and held her gaze. "I'm so happy to have you each on the *Tabitha*." Her eyebrows went up, and Lawrence was glad he'd at least have something to talk about with her once they went out.

FIVE

MAIZEE COULD LISTEN to Lawrence talk about the sea, and lines, and boat etiquette for hours. He had a smooth, round, deep voice that vibrated in all the right places inside her body. She gripped her water bottle while he finished up, and then turned back to Kara.

"I didn't know it was a private tour," she said. "How much do I owe you?"

"Oh, this guy is cheap," Kara said with a toss of her dark hair and a nonchalant wave of her hand. "Nan arranged it all, but I think it was only a couple of hundred dollars."

Maizee nodded like that made total sense to be on this luxury sailboat with a billionaire banker as the captain. But Kara nor Nan nor anyone else knew who he was, obviously. And he wanted to keep it that way.

She liked that they had a little secret together, and her hand still buzzed from where his had held it.

She moved over to Nan and asked her about the price.

"Oh, it was only a hundred and fifty," she said. "So divide that by seven, and it's what? Twenty bucks? Don't worry about it."

Nan obviously came from money too—at least a little—because she wore designer clothes to go sailing. Maizee felt underdressed in a simple sundress, and she wished she'd brought an oversized hat like a couple of the other women.

She felt Lawrence's eyes on her, and she turned toward him. Sure enough, he watched her as he worked one of the lines, and everything in her got set to boil. There were too many pieces of him, and Maizee didn't know how to put them all together into a complete puzzle.

He hiked in the rain. Saved women. Stayed with them until they were safe. Wore power suits to work. Went into the ritziest hotel with men like him. And sailed his boat for pennies.

Nothing about him made sense, and Maizee really wanted to dig deeper into him and find out more about him. Learn what made him tick.

She wanted complicated if it came with Lawrence Gladstone.

But she didn't go over to him. She chatted with the other women and let the ocean breeze blow her hair off her face and shoulders. She enjoyed the pear and gorgonzola tarts Lawrence served, and went back to the soda bar over and over again for one of his delicious flavored concoctions.

She flirted with him shamelessly, only when no one else was looking, and he didn't seem to mind.

"There were whales out here earlier," he said once he'd pulled in the sails and the boat started drifting. "But I don't see them now. They often feed in the morning, though we do see them at all times of the day out here."

He sounded like a tour guide, but the kind she could eat lunch with as he educated her about the island. He was windswept, wearing a pair of khaki shorts and a tank top that showed he spent plenty of time taming sails. Or lifting weights. Anything but sitting behind his desk in that second-floor office in the corner.

Who knew? Maybe he lifted weights up there and she just didn't know it yet.

He told them a bit about the aquatic life here, but they didn't see any before he set the sails again and put them on a course back toward land.

The sun was arcing toward the west when he finally docked the boat, and Maizee's stomach grumbled for dinner. Could she ask him out? Would he go? If he said no, how could she look him in the face come Monday morning?

She hung back as the other women disembarked, until it was just her and Lawrence left on the *Tabitha*.

"So, did you enjoy yourself?" he asked, working to secure the boat. "Have you ever been sailing before?"

"Lots of times," she said. "I grew up on the island of Lanai."

"Oh," he said, keeping his eyes on his work. "That's great."

"But this was amazing," she said. "We don't have our own boat. We'd just rent little ones for the day or go sea kayaking."

"Sea kayaking?" Their eyes met, and Maizee actually fell

back a step from the electric current running between them. "That sounds dangerous."

"It's actually really fun," she said. "And East Bay has some great currents."

"You've been?"

"Not yet, but I've been reading up on the best places to go here."

"You have your own sea kayak?" He moved down to a new line and began reeling it in, tightening it like a real pro would on a sailboat.

"Yes," she said, feeling a bit defensive and then a bit sad. "But it's at home, on Lanai."

He nodded. "I'm not what you'd call an outdoorsy guy."

"No?" She tilted her head to look at him closer, but he didn't meet her gaze this time. "You were hiking when we first met."

"Yeah, well, that's a loose term for what I was doing."

"What were you doing then?"

He took several long seconds to answer, and when he finally did, it was only with, "Exploring."

Maizee wasn't sure what that meant. "You're a great sailor."

"Thank you." He grinned at her and time seemed to stall completely. "Listen, this might be…I don't know. I've been thinking about you since last weekend. Would it be weird if we went to dinner or something?" His dark eyes sparked with intensity, with hope, and Maizee felt a smile fill her whole soul, her whole face.

"I'd like to go to dinner with you."

"I don't normally date anyone who works for me," he

said, swallowing as if he was the nervous one. "If it's too weird, I get it."

"It can't be weirder than a billionaire pretending to be a sailboat tour guide." She bumped him with her hip, surprised at her own boldness. After all, he *was* her boss.

But he laughed, the sound dangling in the air like musical chimes, sweet and wonderful and making Maizee giggle too.

"Tonight?" she asked when they both quieted. "Or are you busy after this?"

"No," he said, drawing the word out. "You want to go to dinner right now?"

"Sure," she said, her flirtation game thriving. "I'm starving."

He glanced around as if she'd been talking to someone else. "Then I just need to finish up here, and we can go."

"Did you want to change?"

"Did you want me to change?"

Maizee quite liked him in whatever he wore, so she shrugged. "Up to you."

Lawrence finished with one more line, and then he said, "I've got clothes downstairs. I'll change and meet you on the dock."

"Sounds great." Maizee wanted to stay and ask him another question, flirt with him under the setting sun. But she knew when to make an exit, and it was now, when he wanted her to stay. She walked across the deck and swung her leg over the side of the boat, climbing carefully down the few steps on the ladder until she reached the dock.

Only then did the bird's wings explode in her chest. A

moan leaked out of her mouth, and she thought, *What in the world are you doing?*

He's your boss!

No, he owns the whole blasted company!

If things "got weird" with him and they broke up, Maizee wouldn't be able to simply transfer to another Gladstone Financial branch.

She'd be out of a job completely.

———

Maizee actually left the dock, thinking she'd just head on home. Lawrence didn't have her number, and she could barricade herself behind her front door. He wouldn't look up her personal information anyway. She wasn't sure why she thought that, only that he seemed like the kind of guy who'd realize what had happened when he disembarked and found her gone.

They could go on pretending not to see one another when he walked right by her glassed in office, and she could figure out the timing of his schedule so their paths didn't cross.

Worry gnawed at her stomach, making it more upset than it already was that she'd underfed it.

She wandered along the tree line that bordered the parking lot at the dock, her car still calling to her. Begging her to get behind the wheel and drive until she figured things out. She avoided it, clenching her phone in her fist, startling when it chimed.

Had to be one of her sisters, and Maizee seized onto the

idea. She could call Evelyn and ask her—hypothetically, of course—about dating the owner of the company. Evie would know what to do.

But when she lifted her phone and looked at it, the message was not from Evelyn or Juliet. It was an unknown number, and it read *Where did you go? This is Lawrence by the way. I called my secretary to get your number.*

Before she could tap out a single letter of a response, another message came in. *I'm not a stalker. I'm just hungry, and you looked so great in that dress.*

Maizee's stomach settled with such a sweet message, and she turned back to the docks. *Went for a quick walk,* she texted back. *Trying to work my ankle a little bit.*

It wasn't entirely a lie. She did like to give her ankle a workout every few hours, otherwise it stiffened up and caused her pain.

I can meet you at my car.

Maizee didn't need to ask which one was his. Only a handful of cars remained in the parking lot, and only one of them looked like it cost six figures.

I see it. Meet you there. She added a little limp to her left step as she approached his midnight blue Mercedes-Benz. It was sleek and stylish, and she supposed it was meant to show others that Lawrence was strong and not to be trifled with.

He sidled up beside her, and said, "Hey."

When Maizee looked at him, she found a strong, masculine man who also happened to wear a sexy meekness right on his face.

"Still starving?" he asked.

"Yes, sir."

Their eyes met, and Maizee ducked her head, a giggle coming out of her mouth even though she was much too old for such sounds.

"How's your ankle?" he asked, ignoring both the comment and the girlishness. "I saw you limping."

"It's good sometimes and then it hurts a little sometimes." Maizee lifted one shoulder in a shrug, noticing that Lawrence's gaze lingered there.

"What do you like to eat?" he asked.

"Pretty much anything," she said, her pulse swinging around in her chest like a pendulum. She couldn't remember ever feeling this excited about a date with Winn, and she'd kept an eye on him for six months before he'd asked her out.

Lawrence had only taken seven days, and Maizee liked that. Maybe he'd been wrestling with his feelings too.

"I know a great Polynesian place," he said, reaching past her to open the door. "Sound good?"

"Absolutely," she said. "My mother makes a killer poi."

He smiled at her, his teeth as straight and white as only good money could make them. She dropped down into his car, glad she hadn't worn heels and wondering how she'd ever get out of this car even wearing her flats.

He sauntered around the front of the car, and she drank in the dark slacks he'd changed into. The sky blue shirt, open at the throat, with a suave jacket over that. No tie. No cufflinks. Windblown hair.

He was devastatingly gorgeous, and Maizee wondered—again—what in the world she was doing with him. What she really wanted to know was what he saw in her.

He got in the car, and she noticed he wore loafers, not his shiny leather shoes. Everything about him said casual in a very extravagant way. The car started with a roar and then a purr, and he said, "So let's start with basics. I know it's impolite to ask a woman her age, so I'll start and you can say older or younger." He cut a glance at her out of the corner of his eye. "I'm forty-one."

Maizee may have looked up some information on him throughout the years, and she was ready to say, "I'm just younger than that."

"Ever been married?" he asked.

"No. You?" she asked, though she knew he hadn't. The marriage of Lawrence Gladstone would be the event of the century, wouldn't it?

"No, ma'am."

"Ever been close?"

"Not even a little bit." His fingers squeezed the steering wheel. "You?"

Maizee waited for him to make a right turn, and then she said, "Yes, actually. I was engaged before moving here." She didn't say that her failed engagement was the reason she'd left Lanai and come to Getaway Bay, but Lawrence was a smart guy. He could hear the words behind what she did say.

"Not wearing a ring now," he said. "Any chance of that rekindling?"

Maizee laughed and shook her head, her hair tickling her bare arms. "Not even a little bit."

He smiled at her, pulled into a restaurant that was bursting at the seams, and parked right at the curb.

"Oh, I don't think—" Maizee cut off when someone opened her door. A man in a uniform stood there, someone she hadn't even seen. Now, the two dozen people milling outside the restauarant were definitely visible.

"Hello, Mister Lawrence," the man said even as he extended his hand to help Maizee from the car. "Two tonight?"

"Yes, Kael. Thank you."

Maizee used Kael's strength to help her stand, holding onto his hand while her weak ankle adjusted to holding her weight. Before she could let go, he passed her to Lawrence, who had come around the car to the sidewalk.

"Right this way, sir." Kael led them right through the throng, and Maizee's senses felt like they would cause her head to explode. The scent of delicious food and Lawrence's cologne. The feel of his hand in hers had every cell in her body firing on all cylinders. The way the onlookers watched as she and Lawrence walked right past them and inside the clearly busy restaurant.

Kael stepped over to the hostess and spoke a few words Maizee couldn't hear. He returned a moment later and said, "Katia will take you back, sir."

"Thanks," Lawrence said again, and even though Maizee was busy taking in every little detail around her, she noticed him press a tip into Kael's hand before they followed Katia back to a private table in the corner.

She sat across from him, hoping she wasn't about to make the worst mistake of her life.

SIX

LAWRENCE WISHED he would've remembered it was a Saturday night at La Coconut. If he had, he would've taken Maizee somewhere else. Somewhere a little quieter, a little more off the beaten path.

Having to walk through all those waiting customers like he owned the place hadn't helped, as she was now looking at him like he owned the world. While he was used to such things, he certainly didn't want it to come from her.

"We can go somewhere else," he said.

"Are you kidding?" She unwrapped her silverware and spread her napkin on her lap. "I've never been here, and it smells delicious." She looked around, obviously admiring the plates of the diners around them.

"Where have you been on the island?" he asked.

"Roasted," she said. "And the grocery store."

"Ah, so you cook." He looked up at the waiter, who

carried a bottle of wine. "None for me, thank you." He glanced at Maizee.

"Just water for me," she said, and Lawrence's humiliation over not being a drinker fled. He grinned at her again as she said, "I don't necessarily cook. But I like to bake."

"Oh, yeah? What do you make the most?"

"Chocolate cake."

Oh, he was going to be in so much trouble. If she could bake a chocolate cake that tasted anywhere near as good as she looked, he could lose his heart to this woman. He pulled back on his thoughts, as this was their very first date. Just because he hadn't been out with anyone in a long time didn't mean he was ready to get married tomorrow.

His feelings just seemed to stream through him so strongly, and he didn't know how to tame them.

"I'd like to try that," he said. "I'm a sucker for chocolate."

She picked up her menu and started studying it. "Lualua. I'm having that."

"It's one of my favorites too," he said, leaving his menu on the table. He wasn't on a first-name basis with the staff for no reason. "Their poke is also delicious."

Her blue eyes met his over the top of the menu, and wow, he forgot how to breathe.

"Ah, with tuna. Sounds delicious."

He let a few moments of noise pass by. "I don't really believe you."

She set her menu down and laughed. "Yeah, you shouldn't. I don't like raw fish."

"And you grew up in Hawaii?"

"It takes all kinds," she said, folding her arms on the table and leaning into them. "Makes the world interesting, no?"

"Definitely."

The waiter returned, and he gestured for her to order first. She went with the lualua, and Steven asked, "Pork, chicken, or beef?"

"Pork."

"Macaroni salad okay?"

"Yes."

"Poi?"

"Absolutely."

"Fried plantains?"

"Bring it all." She smiled at him, and Lawrence liked her charm, her wit, and her spirit. No wonder she made him feel alive. With a start, he realized he didn't even know he was sort of dead inside until that moment.

"And for you, sir?" Steven looked at him, and Lawrence was glad he got someone who knew how to wait on him. Steven would stop by once after the food was brought, and he'd refill the drinks as he kept an eye on them like a hawk.

"Same as her."

"Yes, sir." He glanced at the table. "No Dr. Pepper tonight?"

"Yes, please. You know how I like it."

Steven nodded and left, and Lawrence wished he had his soda now to hide behind.

"You know how I like it?" Maizee repeated, leaning forward even further. "Do you own this place, Lawrence?"

He blinked at her and then laughed. "Heavens, no."

"What's he going to bring you?"

"A Dr. Pepper with cherry and coconut."

"Ah, like you were making on the boat." She sat back, the playfulness in her eyes unlike anything he'd seen at the office.

"Yeah," he said. "I like a fun flavored soda." He liked the burn of the carbonation down his throat, and the way the caffeine zipped through his system.

"What else do you like?" she asked. "Fruity Dr. Pepper and chocolate cake." She ticked the two items off on her fingers. "Sailing. Finance." She stalled, watching him.

"Sandwiches," he said. "If you can put it on bread or a roll, I'm sold."

She trilled out a laugh, tucking her hair behind her ears, something Lawrence had the crazy craving to do too. But he would not be touching her again tonight. He was certain the only reason she'd let him hold her hand as they walked into the restaurant was because Kael had set it all up. The hundred dollar bill Lawrence had given him wasn't even close to enough.

"What about you?" he asked. "You like…." He didn't want to list anything, because he wasn't confident in getting them right. "Baking. Coffee. Sea kayaking. Paperwork."

She groaned and shook her head. "Paperwork? Who likes paperwork?"

"Loan officers," he said, grinning at her. Steven brought their drinks and made himself scarce, and as the conversation continued, Lawrence learned that Maizee liked almost anything she could do outdoors: hiking, sailing, kayaking, hammocking, and lying on the beach.

So pretty much the opposite of him making his dirty Dr. Pepper and collapsing on the couch to watch his streaming service. She did like her job, but definitely not the paperwork part of it, and she definitely didn't eat anything in the breakfast food family.

The lualua was delicious, and Lawrence cleaned his plate, glad when Maizee did too. When it was time to leave, he threw a few bills on the table and stood, expecting her to move in front of him.

Instead, she reached for his hand and he slipped his fingers between hers effortlessly, wondering if they should talk about this growing attraction between them. Did they need to, because they worked together? He didn't need drama in the branch, and as they waited on the curb for Kael to get his car, Lawrence tugged her a little closer to him.

"What are you thinking about this?"

"About what?"

"Us." When she didn't answer, he said, "I'm particularly concerned about what you want from me while we're at work."

Kael pulled up and the conversation stalled while he opened doors for them, received another tip, and Lawrence pulled away from the still-busy restaurant.

"What do you want from me at work?" she asked.

Lawrence thought about the question as he navigated back to the dock, where she'd left her car. He parked beside her and looked out the windshield. "I think you're beautiful, and I had a great time tonight."

"Thank you," she said. "I did too."

"Would it hurt your feelings to ask that we kept our relationship…private for the time being?" He turned to look at her, needing to judge her expression in this moment.

"That's fine," she said, and it might've been the first time a woman said something was fine and meant it.

"I don't like drama at the bank," he said. "And honestly, I'm still trying to decide if I've made a huge mistake or not."

Maizee looked like he'd splashed ice water in her face, but she recovered quickly. "I know what you mean."

"Do you?"

"The man I was engaged to?" She heaved a sigh and looked out her window. "He was the branch manager in Lanai. When we broke up, I couldn't go back to work. I asked for a transfer immediately, and well." Another sigh, and Lawrence strongly disliked this unsettled side of Maizee. "That's why I'm here now, and not there."

Lawrence wanted to reach across the console and take her hand in his. But he asked, "You were engaged to Winthrop Porter?"

She swung her attention to him. "Yes. You know him?"

"He's my branch manager on Lanai," Lawrence said. "Of course I know him." And he didn't like him much, though he did a great job in the branch. But what in the world had Maizee seen in him?

"So we'll just play things by ear," he said quietly. "No romance in the office. And if things get weird for either of us, we'll say." He searched her face, realizing he could easily lose himself in this woman's blue-eyed gaze. "Okay?"

She nodded. "Okay."

"Great." He smiled. "So what are you doing tomorrow?"

———

Lawrence spent the morning at the sporting goods store, buying anything and everything he could think of that one might need to bike down the coast and spend the day on the beach. He had backpacks, sunscreen, towels, an umbrella, a bike, helmet, and enough clothes to keep him cool and dry for a week.

He loaded up everything he could fit in his car, and he asked if he could get the bike delivered to his building by noon. Of course he could, because he could pay anyone to do anything when he wanted them to.

So it was that he was standing on the sidewalk, properly geared up, a stylish backpack on his back and standing beside the best bike money could buy, when Maizee showed up. She wore tight spandex from shoulder to knee, and she rode her bike like a professional.

Lawrence's heart beat out of control, and he blurted, "I'm not going to lie. I can't remember the last time I rode a bike."

Maizee laughed, a musical sound that increased his pulse, and said, "Did you buy that bike this morning?"

"I sure did."

She tipped her head back and laughed again, filling the sky with the sound of it. "Why didn't you just say so?"

He shrugged. "You said you liked biking to a picnic spot. I figured I could do it, even though the last time I rode a bike, I was twelve years old."

"How did you get around?" she asked.

"The subway," he said. "New York City sidewalks aren't kind to bicyclists."

Maizee shook her head, a look of admiration on her face. "It's flat, hard ground," she said. "Maybe twelve miles. And I brought all the food, even that chocolate cake I mentioned last night."

"All right. You go first." He didn't want her to watch him try to get on the bike, something he hadn't even done yet. But he did want to do things he hadn't before, and if he could ride behind the beautiful Maizee Phelps to a picnic on the beach, he was going to do it.

She kicked off easily, and he managed to get himself on the bike without falling down. Why couldn't riding a bike be as simple as reading a financial document or converting currency? Those things he could do.

But with every stroke of the pedal, things got a little better. The view was gorgeous, with the ultra-blue ocean on his right and the rolling green hills of Hawaii on his right. He followed Maizee until she turned off the road onto a sandy path, and then he dismounted. She chained her bike to a tree, and he followed suit, thinking he'd probably follow this woman wherever she wanted to go.

Once again, he forced himself not to think too far ahead. This was a fun Sunday afternoon date with a woman he was just getting to know. He may very well learn things about her he didn't like, and then he'd have to decide what to do.

But for now, he took her hand yand tromped through the sand in his new biking shoes to a designated spot. She spread out a blanket and pulled out a few bags of food, perfectly chilled with pockets in the side she'd filled with ice packs.

Lawrence loved the salty scent of the sea as it mixed with Maizee's perfume, and he was glad to be outside for probably the first time in years. He felt brave, indestructible, and like he was really living his life.

Finally.

SEVEN

MAIZEE CAUGHT Lawrence's eye as he passed her office and started up the stairs to his. He didn't wave. Or smile. Nothing. He did nothing. Just continued past.

Though they'd talked about it, and she'd expected him to do exactly what he'd done, her chest still pinched.

They'd had *such* a great weekend together. Sunday afternoon had passed in the blink of an eye, ending with her curled into his side as the sun sank into the ocean. She'd confessed that sunsets were some of her favorite times of the day, and he'd laughed at her while she ate her cake before the rest of her lunch.

The conversation had been light and easy, nothing about Winn or previous relationships. Nothing serious about how they'd act at work. Just enjoying the sand, the surf, and the sun—and each other.

He'd told her that his sailboat was named after his

grandmother, and she liked the vulnerability he showed when he spoke of the important people and things in his life.

She felt a bit windblown and sunburnt this morning, but it wasn't anything a little moisturizer and a lot of makeup couldn't fix.

Her phone sizzled at her, and she made a grab for it as she'd set that notification specifically to Lawrence. *Morning, beautiful.*

Good morning yourself, she sent back, glad she hadn't been out of the dating game for too long. Lawrence possessed a quiet spirit, and he was completely unlike the man she'd imagined the owner of Gladstone Financial to be.

Yes, he was gorgeous. Strong. Wealthy. But he had a soft side. A vulnerable side, and he had confessed that he was working on doing things around the island that he'd previously never experienced. Thus, the hiking last weekend and the bike-riding this one.

She liked that he was willing to try new things, but that those same things made him nervous.

He had become more human to her over the course of the last two days, and while she still imagined him to be able to do anything, at least she knew some of it made his nerves fly into overdrive.

I have a lunch appointment today, his next message said. *But I'm free for dinner.*

She giggled and immediately glanced toward her open door. But no one ever came to see her this early in the morning. After all, no one had *go to the bank* as their first errand of the day, and her afternoons were always busier than her mornings.

Are you asking me out? she thumbed out and sent just as Will walked into her office. She glanced up and erased the smile from her face. "Good morning, Mister McMahon. What can I do for you?"

He glanced over his shoulder and entered her office before closing the door behind him. He took the seat across from her as her phone sizzled again. She swiped quickly to silence it, wishing she could continue her flirtatious texting with Lawrence.

She met Will's eye again and this time she did flash him a tight smile. He sat there, his gaze appraising and firm, and she fought the urge to squirm. She'd only been at this branch for a week. What could've possibly gone wrong?

And why did she care? Anyone could process loans, and Maizee had been seriously considering her life choices over the course of the past few days. Well, not on Saturday during the sailing, nor Sunday during the picnic. But before that.

"I need a loan," he finally said, and surprise mingled with relief in her lungs.

"Well, you've come to the right place." She opened a drawer and pulled out the employee applications for loans. "We have the best rate for employees out of any other bank." Maizee slipped into her salesperson voice, pointing at boxes on the form, and then the website address at the bottom. She told Will she would put his to the top of the pile if he went with the paper application, or watch for his email if he used the website.

He grew redder and redder during the brief conversation, and then he stood, leaving the paper on the desk. "Thank you, Maizee," he said.

She stood and stepped around the desk. "Of course."

Will opened the door and walked out without looking back. Maizee caught the door before it could clang into the glass and watched him go. She wasn't sure what he was playing at. Was he testing her? Seeing how she'd treat an employee who came in asking for a loan? Or did he truly need the money?

No matter what, she'd been professional and courteous, and there was no way he could find fault with what she'd done.

Still, something gnawed at her as he disappeared into his office, and she let herself wonder what her life would be like if she'd gone to pastry school or perhaps taken up beach volleyball as a profession. But the required bikini as a uniform was just a bit out of her reach.

Turning back to her desk, she caught sight of her phone screen brightening, and she hurried back over to it.

Lawrence had texted a few times. First with, *Yes, I'm asking you out.*

We can do something totally American. Burgers out at Cattleman's Last Stop.

If you want.

Oh, Maizee wanted to go to dinner with him. She wasn't sure where Cattleman's Last Stop was, but she did like a juicy hamburger with all the toppings. She sent back, *I'm in. You want to come pick me up tonight?*

They'd met for both of their dates so far, though she suspected the ritzy high-rise where she'd picked him up yesterday afternoon was really his home. He probably owned the whole block.

Definitely. Text me your address. I'm headed out for the day.

Sure enough, about five minutes later, Lawrence walked past her office, the sight of his back in his dark suit almost as tantalizing as watching him enter the bank.

She wanted to jump up and follow him, find out where he was going. But he didn't answer to anyone at this bank; he simply happened to have an office here because he enjoyed living in Hawaii. At least that's what he'd told her while they lay on the sand together last night.

He liked being in a time zone behind New York City, as he could make more practical decisions after the heat of the moment was over.

Maizee stayed at her desk, but it took a great deal of will power. She ate lunch at her desk, as she had every day last week. And she left the bank right when the clock struck five so she could rush home and get ready for her dinner date.

She brushed invisible lint from her skirt right as the doorbell rang. Lawrence had obviously found her house, and her heart vibrated the way the sound of the bell still did.

Taking a deep breath, she told herself, "Go have fun." At the same time, tremors moved through her stomach. She couldn't believe she was going out with another man from her bank. The risk she was taking seemed astronomical, and it accounted for at least half of her nerves as she walked down the hall to answer the door.

Lawrence stood there in a button-up shirt the color of raspberries, which he'd paired with a pair of black shorts that shone like oil in the evening sunlight. He glanced up from his phone like he was waiting for the bus, and then his hands fell to his sides.

His eyes raked across her body from top to bottom and back again, a hint of desire and hunger entering his expression. He whistled as the heat from outside started to make Maizee melt a little.

"Don't you look amazing?" He stepped into her, and she should've fallen back to allow him room.

She didn't, easily slipping her hand into his as he entered her personal space.

"I love the dress," he murmured, bending his head a bit to sweep his lips along her forehead.

Maizee had bought it for her engagement party and worn it exactly once. It felt good, freeing, to wear it again and receive a compliment from a handsome man. She loved the silvery sheen of it and how sometimes, if the light was just right, it looked blue.

Her stomach growled, and while Lawrence surely couldn't hear it, he stepped back and asked, "Should we go?"

"Yes, I'm starving," she said.

He drove for quite a while, right along the coast and around the curve in the island. Maizee marveled at all the wild land on this island, all the places to explore. She'd make sure she wasn't caught in a rainstorm when she hiked all of this land, and she hoped Lawrence would be with her just in case the sky did open and cause her problems.

The lot in front of the restaurant held quite a few cars, of a wide variety. Pickup trucks, sedans, SUVs, and Lawerence's Benz rounded out the crowd. The tires crunched over the gravel as he found a spot, and he met her at the front of the car and slung his arm around her.

"This ranch is still operational," he said. "They don't send calves to the Mainland, but only produce beef for local consumption."

"Fascinating," she said. "What's it called?" The restaurant had a sign that read "Cattleman's Last Stop," but surely that wasn't the name of the entire ranch.

"Wahine Nani," he said. "It means beautiful woman in Hawaiian. The history says that a Spanish *paniolo* came from California and fell in love with an island princess. They started this ranch, and the land is blessed as long as there are Hawaiian cattle roaming it."

Maizee loved listening to the sound of his voice. "How do you know all this?"

"I like to read."

"An indoor activity."

He laughed as he mounted the steps. "Yes, an indoor activity." He opened the door to a wall of sound but tried to talk over it. "I know a lot about this place, I just haven't gotten out and seen it for myself."

"Well." Maizee moved right into his chest and placed her hand over his heartbeat. Was it her imagination or did his pulse skip around a bit? Did she really have that effect on him? It seemed impossible, as she felt way out of her league. "We're changing all of that, aren't we?" She stepped into the bar and restaurant before he could answer and drank in the surroundings.

The décor was quite tacky, but it somehow fit the theme of a ranch restaurant that served some of the biggest burgers and thick-cut fries Maizee had ever seen. She watched a waitress walk by with three plates balanced in her hands, marveling that she didn't drop them as she stepped.

"Two tonight?" a man asked. He wore a cowboy hat and jeans, and the only indication that he worked there was the apron around his waist, which bore a huge horseshoe with the words *Last Stop* splashed over it. He grabbed two menus and glanced at Lawrence.

"Oh, hey, Larry." He grinned at him. "Haven't seen you in a while."

"Evening, Mack." Lawrence smiled easily at the man and said nothing about the nickname. Maizee gawked at him, his demeanor, clothing, and professional status nowhere near a *Larry*.

But she waited until Mack had tossed the paper menus on the table and sauntered away in his cowboy boots before exclaiming, "Larry?" with a little giggle.

He shrugged one shoulder and lifted the water glass that was already on the table to his lips. "Sometimes I like to be anonymous."

She scoffed. "Does that actually work?"

"Out here, it does." He gazed at her evenly. His eyes positively sparkled when he leaned forward and said, "So be sure to call me Larry."

Wow, his mouth couldn't be any more perfect, all curved up like it was. Maizee's heart was the one skipping around now, and all she could think of was what it would be like to kiss the man sitting across from her.

His lips said, "Dr. Pepper," alerting her to the fact that someone had arrived and had asked for their drink orders.

"Do you ever drink anything besides Dr. Pepper?" she asked.

"Sure," he said, but he didn't specify what.

She tore her eyes from him and said, "I'll have strawberry guava lemonade."

The cowgirl who'd moseyed over left, and Lawrence leaned back in his chair. "So, you're quite sporty. Tell me what else you do. Ziplining? Skydiving?" He didn't wear a smile, and Maizee's chest pinched all the air out of her lungs.

Sporty? What did that mean?

Did he like sporty? Was she too masculine for him? She'd tried to doll herself up with the silver dress, but maybe he thought she was trying too hard.

She gulped her water, trying to figure out how to answer.

And Larry just sat there and stared at her, no help whatsoever.

EIGHT

LAWRENCE HAD OBVIOUSLY SAID something wrong. What, he didn't know. But Maizee sat there, blinking much too fast. Then she started gulping water, which was a real feat as the liquid in his glass tasted like it had come from the animal troughs out on the ranch.

"Sporty?" she finally squeaked.

"Yeah," he said, trying to figure out how she could take that the wrong way. "You do like hiking and biking and stuff." He worked very hard not to pitch his voice up on the end, as if it were a question. He already knew she liked outdoor activities, and that was pretty sporty to him.

"Yes." She finally realized the water wasn't good, because she pushed the glass further from her.

Lawrence didn't want to play games, and frustration rose through him. "So what did I say wrong?"

"Do you find me too sporty?"

"I'm not sure what that means."

"Now you know how I feel."

Lawrence glanced up as their drinks arrived, taking a few moments to center his thoughts. "I don't think you're too sporty," he said before Jane even moved away.

"Are my muscles too big?"

Lawrence blinked. Was that something women worried about? "Of course not."

"Am I too masculine?"

"No."

"I wear too many pant-suits to work."

"Do you?" Lawrence was so confused. He wasn't sure how "sporty" had translated to "masculine" or "you wear too many pant suits to work."

"Then what?" she asked.

Lawrence didn't know how to answer her. "I think you misunderstood me," he said. "I was simply asking what else you liked to do. You seem…to enjoy the outdoors. Doing adventurous things. I don't. That's all."

He suddenly wished he hadn't asked Kaelin and Tyler for dinner conversation topics at that day's Nine-0 meeting. But they were the two most outdoorsy men, and Lawrence could admit when he needed a little help.

In fact, that was what made him so successful at his company. He knew what his strengths were, and what he needed a second or third opinion on. But in this case, maybe he should've just stuck to his own thoughts when it came to what he and Maizee could talk about.

Maizee watched him, her blue eyes intense and still searching his, as if he hadn't spoken the truth.

"You're more adventurous than you think," she finally said.

"How so?"

"I've never gone out as an alternate identity. It's very James Bond of you." She'd returned to her usual, flirtatious self, but Lawrence wasn't sure if she really felt like he'd explained himself well enough. If she really accepted what he'd said.

He wanted to tell her how beautiful he found her, that he'd spent the last several hours contemplating how he could kiss her good-night in just an hour or two, that he'd had to leave work early that day simply so he wouldn't call her up to his more private office and advance their relationship to the next level.

She wasn't ready for that, even if she did flirt with him like there was no tomorrow. That was just Maizee. Blonde, blue-eyed, adventurous, fun Maizee.

The fact that she was a loan officer was a bit of an outlier, actually. "So if you weren't a loan officer, what would you be?" he asked next, a topic he'd thought of all by himself, thank you very much.

"Oh, I don't know," she said airily.

"Yeah, I'm not buying that." Lawrence felt like he was calling her out left and right tonight. But she didn't seem to mind, and he really did want to know deeper level things about her.

"You're not?"

The country music song that had been blaring through the space ended, and Lawrence enjoyed the momentary silence before the next one began. The dance floor was full constantly, but he had no plans to join anyone out there. And if Maizee asked, he'd claim to have broken his leg on the way in.

But she probably wouldn't ask, not with her ankle still healing.

"Fine," she said, pushing out an exaggerated sigh. "When I was younger, I thought about going to pastry school."

He thought about her wearing a white apron and making that chocolate cake day in and day out. "Yeah, you'd be good at that." But it wasn't something that fit her personality, at least not in his opinion.

"I always thought it would be fun to be a tour guide," she said with a little shrug. "Like, at an aquarium or a wild animal park."

Lawrence chuckled. "Is there an aquarium or wild animal park here in Hawaii?"

"We have an aquarium on Lanai," she said. "And submarine tours. That might be fun."

He nodded. Yes, he could see her interacting with people all day long, a smile stuck to her face. A genuine smile.

"You'd probably hate that," she said, glancing around the restaurant. "Wow, they're not very fast here, are they?"

"Not really," he said. "You in a hurry?"

"Yes, I might bite off your arm if I don't get something to eat soon."

Lawrence laughed then, a full belly laugh that rivaled the noise level of the music. He hadn't felt this lighthearted in such a long time, and he'd had no idea his life was so void of humor, or amusement, or well, *life*.

He had his company. His financial pages and magazines and reports. His friends.

But none of them held a candle to Maizee and the joy she'd brought into his life in the simplest of ways.

Their burgers arrived before she could gnaw on his arm, and Lawrence enjoyed the home-grown beef almost as much as the breathtaking woman across from him.

He drove her home and walked her to the door, and she turned back to him as if she'd invite him in, brew some coffee, and they'd continue to chat for a while.

Then she said, "Thanks, *Larry*. I had fun." She grinned at him, opened the door with her back to it, and stepped up into the house without taking her eyes from his.

"Me too," he said, knowing he shouldn't follow her in, and that there would be no kissing tonight. "See you tomorrow."

He tucked his hands in his pockets and went down the steps and on back to his car. He wasn't frustrated, only disappointed. But Lawrence didn't give up after his first attempt at anything. Just like he would conquer that hike up to the Umauma Falls, he would give Maizee as much time as she needed to realize that she wanted to kiss him as much as he wanted to kiss her.

———

"So it's true then?" Lexie Keller—now Burnes that she'd married Jason—lined up her shot and hit the ball off the tee.

She faced him, her long, dark hair hanging over her arms. "You're *dating* someone?"

Lawrence refrained from rolling his eyes. Lexie's family had also been in New York finance, and he thought his father still wanted him to marry someone like her. Someone with their own money, and financial breeding, and all that stuff. But Lawrence found himself quite boring, and he couldn't imagine being with someone like Lexie.

She was nice, sure. Professional. Smart as a whip. But he wasn't excited by her, not in the slightest.

"You don't have to say it like it's never happened before," he said.

"Well, I'm not sure it has." She stepped out of the way so her husband could take his turn. They weren't actually golfing, but just hitting balls out into a course that would give them points. Lawrence only kept up his golf game on the off-chance his father would show up one day and want to talk business.

He'd long claimed that the best business decisions were made on greens, and Lawrence felt he should be ready should his dad ever want to take him out on the course. But neither of his parents had come to Hawaii once since Lawrence had moved here years ago, and he wasn't all that sorry about it.

He kept the company humming along, and his dad traveled other parts of the world during his retirement, a new woman at every destination. His mother had given up a decade ago in her questions about when Lawrence would find a wife and start having grandchildren for her.

Thankfully, his two younger sisters had filled that need

for his mother, and she lived near the two of them in Maryland. He had six nieces and two nephews he rarely saw, and a twinge of guilt seemed to be ever-present in the back of his mind.

Lexie peered at him as Jason's club made a cracking sound against the ball. The other man grunted and turned back to them with a disgruntled look on his face. Lawrence liked Jason a lot—he was low-key, casual. Lawrence didn't have to be "on" around Jason, didn't have to know everything about every mutual fund, every stock price, every conversion rate.

He picked up his drink and sucked half of it down. "I'm no good at golf."

Lawrence chuckled and ignored Lexie's pointed look as he waved his club in front of the sensor that would spit out a ball for him. He bent and put it on the tee as Lexie said, "Well, do we get to know her name?"

"You know I'm dating someone," he said, glancing at her, wondering if Maizee would categorize a few meals as dating. "You're telling me your spies are so bad they couldn't provide you with a name?"

He quirked his eyebrows and waited for her to answer. She glared instead, and Lawrence hit his ball, watching it fly straight toward the far target and bounce in for eight points. He waved his club to get another ball.

"It's probably a mistake anyway," he said. "Probably won't last."

"Why would you say that?" Lexie stepped over to him so he couldn't swing. "I've never understood why you don't always have a girlfriend."

"Women are…." Work. Maintaining a relationship took work, and Lawrence had always wanted his focus on his company, not his heart. In fact, he could risk almost any amount of money, but he couldn't seem to put his heart on the line. He never had, because he'd seen enough men with broken pieces strung from ocean to ocean. His father, for one. And Lawrence didn't need his fortune split four ways, between four wives he didn't speak to anymore.

No, he wasn't going to follow in those particular footsteps of his father's.

"Women are what?" Lexie pressed.

"Work," Lawrence said truthfully. "And I've always had plenty of that to do somewhere else."

"So what's different about this one?" she asked.

"I'm not sure." Lawrence gestured her back so he could take his next shot, the white lie burning his tongue. He smacked the ball, but it shanked to the left, and he turned and put his club back in the bag. "She's adventurous. She does things I've never thought about doing."

"Like what?" Jason asked, everyone apparently giving up on the golf. Relief flowed through Lawrence as he sat at the table, the air conditioning blowing over him and the waiter arriving with his nachos.

"Sea kayaking," he said.

"You have a yacht," Lexie said. "You're not afraid of the ocean."

"I am when I'm in a sea kayak," he said. "Yachts are huge. Kayaks are not." He picked up a cheese-laden chip and popped it into his mouth. The ooey, gooey texture made him groan, and he was glad he'd taken today off from the bank.

He figured he'd give Maizee a break. A chance to think without him in her face, on her phone, or anywhere she knew about.

"I met her hiking," he said once he'd swallowed.

"I didn't know you hiked," Lexie said.

"I don't," he said. "I was trying something new, and it started raining, and yeah. There she was." She had been the only human being around, seemingly in the whole world. He didn't want to admit it quite yet, but he felt like she'd rescued him that day on the trail, not the other way around.

"So it was recent," she said. "It rained, what?" She glanced at Jason.

"How should I know?" He grinned at her. "You're the one who memorizes stuff like that."

"With Tropical Storm Eric," she said. "Last weekend."

"Right," Lawrence said. "So it's still really new, and…." He hesitated before saying much more. But Lexie had gotten word that he'd eaten with someone at the Cattleman's Last Stop. Had he known that, he wouldn't have texted Jason to go golfing this morning.

"And what?" Lexie really didn't want to let anything go today.

Lawrence gave her a glare. "You're really nosy, you know that?"

She laughed and shook her head, though her eyes still watched him like he was the most interesting thing she'd seen that year. "It's just that you *never* date."

"Never?" Lawrence asked.

"Name the last woman you went out with," she challenged.

"Easy," he said. "Her name's Maizee Phelps, and we ate at the Cattleman's Last Stop just last night." He gave her a triumphant smile and dug into his food again.

"Before that," she said. "But I got her name from you." She laughed as Lawrence shook his head, glad for an easy day, for this easy conversation with an old friend.

"I guess that would be Rachael," he said.

"A decade ago," Lexie pointed out, shooting a look at Jason as if her husband cared when Lawrence's last date was.

But it sounded pathetic to him. Had it really been that long? Ten years since a woman had caught his eye. It sounded like forever when he thought about it, and he pushed the numbers out of his head.

"She works with me," he said, watching them both for their reactions.

"So?" Lexie asked when it became apparent that Lawrence wanted her to say something.

"You don't think that will be a problem?" Everyone he'd known who tried a workplace romance ended up in tears.

"Why would it be a problem?" Jason put his arm around Lexie. "I worked for Lexie when we started dating."

"Not the first time," Lawrence pointed out.

"She's still the boss," Jason said. "And she knows it."

Lawrence laughed with his friends, and Lexie had gotten the answers she'd apparently wanted, because the conversation moved on to something else. But Lawrence's mind had seized onto one sentence—*why would it be a problem?*—and he couldn't let go.

Maybe a relationship with Maizee could work, and for the first time in a long time, he returned to his penthouse without the possibility of just collapsing on the couch for the evening.

Oh, no. Tonight, he was going to hike to that waterfall and cross an item off his bucket list.

NINE

MAIZEE DIDN'T SEE Lawrence in the branch all week. She worried that she'd upset him somehow, but she'd been over every detail of their date at the Cattleman's Last Stop, and she couldn't come up with anything.

He'd left her house with a smile, pleasant and gorgeous as always.

So why had he suddenly disappeared from the face of the earth? She didn't dare ask around the branch in case it came across as inappropriate. No one seemed to care when he was there or if he wasn't, and she didn't want any attention on her.

Her head stayed down, and all the loan applications and files were up-to-date and meticulous. Friday afternoon found her playing cards on her computer, the screen tilted so no one could see it. But wow, the Getaway Bay branch was slow, and she was *bored* out of her mind.

She told herself she wouldn't have been upstairs in

Lawrence's office anyway, but just knowing he was in the building made work more exciting.

Not only that, but he hadn't texted her for days either. She wanted to go out with him that night, and she moved another card onto the deck, stewing about what to do.

"Just ask him," she muttered to herself. Maybe that was what he was waiting for. Her to make a move that said she liked him. A dozen floodlights went off in her head, and she scrambled for her phone.

Haven't seen you all week. Are you too busy for dinner tonight?

She could cook. Or order something and take it home. Make dessert. Something low-key and out of the public eye. Did she dare invite him into her house? She hadn't been brave enough to do so on Monday, and maybe that was why Lawrence had backed off a little.

Or maybe he thinks this romance has already fizzled out.

Maizee frowned at her phone, willing him to respond. Respond now. Now.

I'll pick up something tasty and make my famous marbled brownies.

She almost scoffed at the word famous. So her dad liked them. Didn't make them world-reknowned or anything.

Tell me more about the brownies.

Relief rushed through her and she laughed at his text.

Chocolate and caramel, she typed out. *Swirled together and baked. They're great.*

I'll bring the food. Your place?

Sure. Seven?

See you then.

Maizee relaxed into her chair, her breath leaving her body. She'd done it, and he was coming over that night.

Sudden panic hit her, and she stood abruptly. "I have to clean my house." The clock on her computer read three-thirty, and she knew the next hour and a half were going to be torture.

———

It was only six-forty-five when someone knocked on the door. Maizee had been scrubbing the kitchen, the floors, and the bathroom since the moment she walked in. She wiped her hair out of her face and turned toward the door, listening.

The doorbell rang this time, and she ripped her yellow rubber gloves off and tossed them into the nearest cupboard —which happened to hold plates, not cleaning supplies. She didn't care. She could deal with them later, when there wasn't a handsome man on her doorstep.

She ran her fingers through her hair, giving it a little fluff before opening the door. But it wasn't Lawrence on the stoop.

"Oh," she said at the same time the Polynesian man said, "I have two pizzas for Maizee?" He started to open his insulated bag before she answered. "Barbecue chicken and Hawaiian with Alfredo sauce."

"Yes," she said, though she had no idea what type of pizza Lawrence had ordered. She took the boxes, signed the receipt, and retreated into the house.

It smelled like antiseptic and cheese, and she hurried to

put away the vacuum before dashing down the hall to make sure her hair and makeup still looked presentable.

The next time a knock sounded on the door, it was precisely seven o'clock, and Lawrence looked so dreamy and delicious that Maizee sighed into the doorframe and just stared at him.

"Hey," he said, seemingly unfazed by the sight of her. "Did the pizza arrive?"

"Yes." She gathered her wits about her and stepped back. "Come on in. I'm just about to start the brownies."

He moved into her house, and the anxiety about having such a high profile man in her humble abode almost made her shove him right back out. He didn't even glance around, but kept his gaze right on hers.

"I'm sorry, what?" she asked, blinking to try to get her brain to work.

"The brownies? You haven't even started them?"

"They're best warm," she said, moving into the kitchen. "But we can eat first." She opened the cupboard to get out the plates and promptly slammed it shut again at the sight of the yellow cleaning gloves.

"I don't feel like doing dishes," she said, heat rushing to her face. "Let me see if I have paper plates." She dug around in a drawer, though she knew exactly where they were. But she stole a few seconds with her head ducked below the counter so she wouldn't have to look Lawrence in the face.

"Here they are." She straightened and tossed the package of paper plates on the counter. "Drinks?" She nearly ripped the door off the cupboard before she remembered she needed plastic.

"Maizee," Lawrence said, and everything in her quieted. She turned toward him, soaking in the heated way he gazed at her. "What's going on?"

"Did I upset you the other night?" she blurted, unsure of where the words had come from. She'd been over it and over it.

"No," he said simply, even tucking his hands into his pockets to complete the picture of *perfectly relaxed billionaire, just standing here in the kitchen.*

"You haven't been in to work since." She didn't mean to accuse him, but he really hadn't been in to work, and he hadn't texted to say why. "I mean, I'm not your boss, so it's none of my business."

Maizee felt near tears, and she didn't even know why. She liked Lawrence too much already, that was probably why. Her emotions seemed to be on a roller coaster, and she didn't know if she wanted to go up or if the fall would hurt her too badly.

Lawrence put a smile on his face that could melt glaciers and stepped over to her. He took her into his arms with ease, like he'd done it countless times before. But he hadn't. This was the first time he'd held her close to him like this, and Maizee wanted the moment to slow, to stop, so she could memorize how warm, and safe, and wonderful she felt standing in the circle of his arms.

"I didn't feel like working this week," he said, his mouth so very close to her ear. His breath washed down her neck, making her shiver. He chuckled, as if he knew exactly how her cells were rioting, knew exactly how he made her feel like she was the only woman in the world, like he knew the effect he had on her and he liked it.

"I don't believe that," she said. "You love your job and your company."

"Yes, I do." He drew in a deep breath of her hair and swayed with her. "But even I need a break sometimes."

"I don't like my job," she whispered as she laid her cheek against his chest and brought her arms around him. She'd never said it out loud, though something had been teeming inside her for a while now.

"You're very good at it."

She inhaled the cottony fresh scent of his shirt. Yes, she was good at her job. "I suppose I am."

"Why don't you do something else?" He stroked her hair, and Maizee wondered where this was all going. If she quit, she wouldn't be dating her boss anymore, but what would she do instead?

"I don't know," she said, releasing him and stepping back. He let her go, the moment broken. Her skin buzzed like it could still feel his hands on her, and she sighed. "Let's eat."

"Okay," he said, flipping open one of the pizza boxes. "I'm not a traditionalist when it comes to pizza. Hope these are okay."

"They're great." Surely he'd called one of her sisters and found out that barbecue chicken pizza was one of her favorites. And this one looked amazing, with big chunks of chicken and thinly sliced red onions. She took two pieces of that and opened her fridge to pull out a case of Dr. Pepper.

"It's probably not very cold yet," she said. "I bought it on the way home from work."

He took two cans and a plastic cup while she got out the ice. They danced around each other in her kitchen until Lawrence finally said, "You didn't have to clean up for me."

"I—"

"I can smell the bleach." He watched her for a moment and then burst out laughing, the last of the awkwardness she'd been feeling drying right up with that glorious sound.

"Stop it," she said, but she started to laugh a bit herself. "Let's go eat outside so we don't asphyxiate." She took her soda and pizza toward the back door. She didn't have a beach view, but a mountain one, which dripped with colorful blooms at this time of year.

"Wow, this is beautiful," he said when he joined her on the back porch. Roger slipped out after him, and while Maizee didn't have a fenced yard, the little dog didn't go far. In fact, he sat at attention at Maizee's feet, just sure he'd get a bite of that chicken. And he wouldn't be wrong.

Maizee ate first, making Roger wait until nearly the end before he got a bite. "I think there's a flower farm up there," she said.

"Yeah," Lawrence said like he knew. "Petals and Leis. I know the guy who owns it."

"Of course you do." She gave him a sly smile, which he thankfully returned. "You didn't grow up here, did you?"

"No, but I've lived here for a while now."

"Do you miss the city?"

"Not even a little bit."

His answer surprised her, but then again, most of what

she'd learned about Lawrence did. "Was it hard to move here?" It had been very difficult for her to leave her family behind, and they were only an island away.

"Not really," he said. "My parents have been divorced for a long time. My dad had just gotten his fourth divorce, and my two younger sisters were married. My mom lives near them, and it was just me in the city."

"Your dad doesn't live there?"

"There wasn't anything or anyone keeping me there." A hint of sadness crept into his voice, and Maizee wanted to comfort him the way he had her in the kitchen. She reached over and touched his knee, the skin-to-skin contact sending a jolt through her.

"I'm sorry," she said, yanking her hand back. She wasn't sure what she was apologizing for—the touch or his family.

He continued eating, and she finished before him and stretched her legs out in front of her.

"I think you should know I haven't dated anyone in a long time." His voice barely met her ears, and it was dead silent in her little neighborhood.

"Oh." It felt impossible that someone like him wouldn't have a date every other night, but at the same time, he felt like the kind of person who waited until he knew what he wanted before making a move.

Maizee's chest tightened. She wanted to make a move, kiss him, let him know she really liked him before he left tonight. Could she do that? The hive of angry bees in her stomach awakened, stinging and stabbing and buzzing the word *Winn, Winn, Winn.*

"How long?" she asked.

"You'd be my first girlfriend in ten years, as my friends pointed out to me earlier this week." He looked at her, his eyes bright and a measure of determination in them.

"Oh, is that what I am? Your girlfriend?" She grinned and nudged him with her shoulder.

"You're not?" he asked, and he was so dang cute.

"Oh, I don't know," she said, enjoying this game. Maizee had always been exceptionally good at flirting. "I think girl-friends kiss their boyfriends, and we haven't done that, so."

Lawrence swallowed, his eyes dropping to her mouth. "At least I know the rules now." He switched his gaze to their surroundings again, saying nothing more.

Maizee stared at him. That was it? He wasn't going to sweep her into his arms and kiss her senseless? She'd practically begged him to. Maybe he didn't want to kiss her.

Well, she wasn't going to ask him again, that was for sure. So she got up and said, "I'm going to grab another piece of pizza. You want anything?"

"No, thank you," he said, his voice back to the near-whisper. Maizee walked away, embarrassment filling her from head to toe.

TEN

YOU WANT ANYTHING?

Yes, Lawrence wanted something very badly, but it was not food. Or Dr. Pepper. Or a spectacular mountain view.

He wanted Maizee, and he wanted her in a way he couldn't even classify. When several minutes went by, and she didn't return, he stood and said to her dog, "Come on, Roger. Let's go inside." The little Jack Russell came with him obediently, and he called, "Maizee?" into her house before entering.

The kitchen was empty, though the pizza boxes were still open and more of the chicken barbecue had been taken. She lived in a quaint place, with plenty of space, high ceilings, and a light blue wash on the walls.

Lawrence liked the way it calmed him and made him feel like he was surrounded by the cottony texture of the sky.

Her living room was neat and orderly, and he hated that she'd felt the need to rush home and tidy up for him. He wanted to see her at her best, her worst, and everything in between. He wanted to know everything about her, the good, the bad, and the ugly.

Roger barked, and Lawrence turned toward the little dog, who stood in the kitchen. "Oh, I'm not feeding you, bud," he said, though Maizee had given him a couple of bites of her pizza. "Where's Maizee, huh?"

Roger cocked his head, and Lawrence felt like an idiot for talking to the dog like it was a human. Then Roger trotted off, heading for the hallway like he'd go get Maizee and somehow apologize for Lawrence too.

Problem was, he wasn't even sure what he'd done wrong. "Obviously something," he muttered, wondering if he was going to get brownies tonight. Maizee hadn't even started them yet, and he knew they took a while to bake and even longer to cool. So his sweet tooth wouldn't be satisfied. The last time he'd left her house, he hadn't been satisfied either. He wouldn't die.

It just felt like it.

"Sorry," Maizee said, breezing into the kitchen with an armful of baking goods. "I forgot I needed more chocolate chips out here." She wouldn't look at him, and she'd gone into Super-Maizee mode, just like she had when looking for the paper plates.

She banged around the kitchen, getting out a mixer and butter and eggs. It was almost painful to watch her, and Lawrence searched his brain for a way he could get her nerves to settle. He wasn't even sure why she was so nervous in the first place.

"What can I do to help?" he asked.

"Nothing," she said, looking in his general direction.

Frustration filled him, and he thought about moving right into her personal space and kissing her right now. Maybe that would get her to settle down and *share* the evening with him. This frantic movement and hurried glances weren't what he wanted.

But he wasn't brave enough to make such a bold move. Did she even want him to? She didn't want to be his girlfriend until he kissed her, she'd said that much. But that didn't mean she was ready for what it would take to wear the label.

So he closed the pizza boxes and stacked them on top of each other, freeing up more counter space for her. He refused to be pushed out of the kitchen though, and he unwrapped the cubes of butter and put them in the bowl.

"What's your favorite dessert?" he asked.

"I don't know."

"I like bread pudding," he said. "There's this shop in New York City that makes it with raspberry sauce and vanilla custard and it is so good."

She measured brown sugar and white sugar and put them in the bowl with the butter. "I like cake," she said.

"All cakes?"

"Chocolate is my favorite."

"Mine too."

Maizee started to settle down a bit, and Lawrence decided he wasn't terrible at small talk. "I'm not a fan of carrot cake," she said. "Unless there are no raisins. Then it's divine."

"You don't like raisins?"

"I don't think they should be in desserts. Just leave the oatmeal cookie alone, you know?"

Lawrence chuckled, glad when Maizee's fun, playful personality started to make a reappearance. She finished putting together the brownies, swirling together the batter and enough caramel to bathe in before sticking the pan in the oven.

"Now, they bake."

"Hmm." He took her into his arms again, and decided to be brave again. "What did I do outside to make you scamper away?"

"Nothing," she said, a little too quickly.

"You're not a great liar." He wanted her right here next to him for a good long while. "You can tell me."

"It'll sound stupid."

"Maizee." He whispered her name and simply acted. His mouth skimmed her forehead and then found her earlobe.

He melted into him, and he kept a firm grip on her waist. "I like you, Maizee," he said, wishing his voice wasn't quite so filled with emotion. "I want to know everything about you." He probably shouldn't vocalize his thoughts, and his heart hammered at him, telling him that if he said these kinds of things, it would end up broken. Shattered.

"I'm…." she said, leaning into his touch as he kissed her right below her ear. Now, if he could just get his mouth closer to hers.

"—scared," she finished. "Remember how I'd just broken up with Winn?"

"Yes," he whispered, pulling away. "But we weren't talking about Winn outside."

"You were talking about me being your girlfriend," she said, her blue, blue eyes coming open to look into his face. He liked this serious, scared version of Maizee almost as much as the fun, flirty one. "And I want that, and it scares me."

So she did want to kiss him. A golden glow started to radiate through him, but he kept his smile from forming fully. "So I messed up because I didn't kiss you?"

"I did open the door for you," she said, a sparkle coming into her expression now. "*Wiiide* open."

"It's just that you…weren't ready on Monday," he said. "And I don't want to push you now. I can wait. I don't have to call you my girlfriend until you're ready." Lawrence was ready, and he honestly wondered if he could do as he'd said and wait.

"Is that why you disappeared this week? Because I wouldn't kiss you on Monday?"

"One of the reasons," he said truthfully. "I know when to back off, Maizee. Honest, I do." He released her and tried to step back, but she held onto him, kept him close.

She looked at him, and he looked right back. Several seconds went by, but Lawrence didn't know what else to say. He felt like he'd laid most of his cards on the table already.

"I like you too," she said.

Lawrence didn't analyze anything. And he didn't hesitate while he found his bravery. He wrapped her in his arms again, leaned down, and touched his lips to hers.

A sigh passed through his whole body, followed immediately by firecrackers and lightning. Wow, he hadn't kissed a woman in a while, and especially not someone like Maizee.

In fact, he was quite sure he'd never kissed someone like Maizee, and he simply couldn't get enough.

He cradled her face in his hands while he kissed her, then moved them through her hair and down her back while he kept kissing her. She matched every movement of his mouth with hers, and it felt like his blood had turned to lava, the flames growing hotter with every stroke.

Before he lost control, he pulled away, his breath coming in bursts and his heart sprinting around his chest. He couldn't tell if it was excited he'd done such a thing, or livid that he'd put it in very real danger of being broken.

It didn't matter. For a kiss like that, he'd risk anything, even his heart.

Her eyes drifted open, and she seemed a bit glazed over still. "Wow," she whispered, and Lawrence wanted to kiss her again.

So he did.

———

Lawrence ignored work—and his phone—for an entire weekend, instead choosing to spend his time with Maizee. She said she wasn't feeling adventurous, so he took them out on his yacht where they wiled away an entire afternoon eating junk food and drinking way too much soda as they lay on their backs and let the autumn sun bake them.

He checked his phone after docking and found yet another text from his father. He made a scoffing noise of disgust, and Maizee said, "What's up?"

"Just my dad," he said, shoving his phone in his back

pocket. He watched the horizon, sort of wishing the day wasn't ending and he could sail back out into the waves. "He's bugging me about a deal, which of course I know about and am handling just fine."

He didn't want to talk about the Austin Exchange. The firm was just big enough to bring in a decent chunk of money, and Lawrence had talked to Daniel Austin earlier that week. He didn't need to bring his father up-to-date on the acquisition, because his father had nothing to do with it.

Maizee wrapped her arms around Lawrence, which made some of his annoyance seep away into the atmosphere. "You won't answer him?"

"I will on Monday," he said, turning to face her. "It's the weekend, and I'm not working every waking minute anymore."

Honestly, Lawrence wasn't sure who he even was anymore. He'd always loved his job, and the mere thought of an acquisition had him salivating and chomping at the bit to push it through. But looking into Maizee's eyes, he wondered if he'd wasted a lot of years focused on the tasks in front of him instead of the *people* in front of him.

And so he didn't answer his father that day, nor on Sunday, when Maizee showed up at his penthouse with more food than two people could possibly eat. And yet, they made sandwiches and put them in backpacks, and she drove them out to some of that wilderness that had piqued her interest when they'd gone to dinner at the Cattleman's Last Stop.

And surprisingly, Lawrence didn't hate walking along a trail barely wide enough for his feet. After getting over the feeling like bugs had invested his skin, it was a lovely walk, with a nice ocean breeze coming in off the water.

And while the sandwiches were just ham and cheese, Lawrence acted like they were fit for royalty. Maizee giggled at him, and said, "I forgot you love sandwiches."

"So much," he said around a mouthful of salty meat and cheese. He swallowed and added, "My mother used to make a fried bologna sandwich. She'd butter both sides of the bread, and put mayo on the inside too. Then one slice of bologna on each piece of bread, with a single slice of cheese between them." He smacked his lips. "Perfection."

She shook her head, smiling all the while. "She grilled it? Like a grilled cheese sandwich?"

"That's right."

"I don't know if I should tell you this…but…I don't like bologna."

Lawrence blinked at her, feigning absolute horror. "Well, I'm sure it's because you've been eating it wrong."

"Eating it wrong?" She sent a laugh heavenward. "What does that even mean?"

He didn't know, and he laughed too, happier than he'd ever been when he rolled onto his back and let his laughter into the sky. And when Maizee collapsed next to him and kissed him, kissed him, kissed him, Lawrence wondered how he'd ever survived a Sunday without her mouth on his.

ELEVEN

AFTER THE MOST PERFECT WEEKEND, with the most perfect boyfriend, Maizee showed up at the bank. Again. It was almost like a dark cloud had descended on her as she drove from her place to Gladstone Financial, Getaway Bay Branch. While the front doors faced the beach, there was no salty spray to be felt, and no breeze to keep her cool.

Just the tellers. The desks. Her glassed-in office where she was supposed to pretend like she was busy.

She thought about another type of glassed-in object—the submarine that went around Lanai and showed people the underwater life up close and personal. She'd told Lawrence she wanted to be a tour guide for an operation like that, and she wondered if Getaway Bay had anything similar.

Surely they must, she thought to herself as she sat at her desk and woke her computer. The Getaway Bay tourism industry had to be two or three times as big as Lanai's, and surely there was something she could do where she wouldn't have to stare at a screen and analyze numbers all day.

She simply hadn't realized that she didn't *want* to stare at a screen and analyze numbers all day. She wished she'd have known that when Winn had broken up with her. Then she could still be on Lanai with her family, maybe with the glass submarine job....

But then you wouldn't have met Lawrence, a voice in her head said, and of course it was right. If she hadn't left Lanai and her family, she'd probably still be wearing sweats at night, eating her way through pints of Ben & Jerry's like they were going out of business and she was going to single-handedly save them.

Lawrence waved to her as he reached the stairs, and she lifted her hand in return. Then she dropped it quickly and glanced around the bank like she'd done a terrible deed. By the time she looked back to the stairs, Lawrence had gone up.

She'd never been in his office, and sudden curiosity burned through her like a flame. Could she invent a reason she needed to go up there and speak to him? Who would even ask?

"This is Maizee Phelps," Polly, another woman who worked at the bank, said. "She can help you with the loan application." She flashed a smile in Maizee's direction and left a couple standing in the doorway of Maizee's office.

She shoved aside her thoughts about Lawrence and jumped to her feet. "Welcome to Gladstone Financial," she said. "Come in and sit down." She grabbed another chair from the back of the room and pushed it close to the one already positioned at her desk.

After closing the door, she rounded her desk and sat down too. "Tell me your names." She smiled like she was most delighted to meet them, and after a few minutes of chit-chatting about Hawaii and the weather and how lucky they were that Tropical Storm Flo had decided to turn, she said, "So, tell me what you're looking for in terms of a loan."

As she helped Barry and Elaine Alsop through the process of refinancing their home, she remembered why she'd liked this job in the first place. She did enjoy interacting with people, liked helping them and ensuring that they were taken care of, liked how powerful and in-charge she felt as she answered questions they didn't know that she did.

Forty minutes later, the Alsop's left with their loan application, and Maizee sat back in her chair, feeling more accomplished than she had in weeks. She wasn't the loser loan officer that had been dumped by the handsome branch manager after a year-long engagement, the woman who hid her face when she went in the grocery store so she wouldn't have to see the pitying looks on people's faces.

She was Lawrence Gladstone's girlfriend, and a good loan officer, and she didn't need to hide her face from anyone.

Turning to check her computer, she caught sight of a man walking her way.

And oh, how quickly she ducked then, definitely hiding her face behind the monitor of her computer. Her stomach swooped and her blood turned to ice.

What in the world was Winthrop Porter doing here?

This was *her* island, and he had no right to be here. Anger simmered in her veins now, melting the ice and encouraging her to lift her eyes above the monitor.

He was gone.

She tried to recall what he'd looked like as he'd walked toward her. Angry? Purposeful? Nervous?

Why had he come from Lanai?

She half-stood at her desk, her calves quivering with the effort it took to perch like that in her heels. "And where did he go?" He wasn't anywhere to be found in the bank that she could see. Not the lobby. Not in line. Not talking to a teller.

Not sitting at someone else's desk.

Which left only one place he could've gone—and that was upstairs.

With trembling fingers, she left her office and approached Polly's desk. She helped customers with new debit cards and opening new accounts. "Did you see that man who just walked in?" she asked. "Tall, sort of blonde, sort of not, blue eyes?"

"Yes, he asked to see Mister Gladstone."

Maizee spun toward the staircase, and it suddenly seemed so ominous. "Did he say why?"

"Said he had an appointment. I pointed him in the right direction." Polly put her hand on Maizee's arm, which caused Maizee to jolt and jump away from her. "Why? Who is he?"

Maizee didn't want to answer. She also didn't want to run into Winn, nor did she want to be in this building while her ex-fiancé and her current boyfriend were chatting. "My ex-boyfriend," she said, downplaying the relationship she'd had with Winn. "Polly, I need to run out for a bit. If anyone comes in for me, will you get their name and number?"

"Sure thing." Polly wore a look of compassion on her face, and she didn't ask another question before Maizee practically bolted for the door.

———

Maizee didn't return to work that day, and Lawrence didn't text. Worry ate at her skin, gnawed at her stomach until she was sure she wouldn't be able to go in tomorrow either.

Maybe Lawrence had truly had some business with Winn.

Maybe neither of them knew she hadn't come back to work.

Maybe Lawrence was simply waiting for her to make the first move again.

So many maybe's, and Maizee didn't want to think about any of them. So she pulled into the theater in town, bought herself a solo ticket to whatever was playing next, and then treated herself to the largest bucket of buttered popcorn available.

The movie didn't do much to distract her, but she did take the leftover popcorn home and turn it into something even more delectable—caramel buttered theater popcorn—with some butter, brown sugar, and marshmallows.

She changed into a pair of yoga pants and a *Back to the Future* T-shirt she'd bought at one of those funny online boutiques. As she stirred the caramel over the popcorn, Roger sat obediently at the no-dogs line, just outside of the kitchen. He didn't even bark, and as Maizee chewed through warm, gooey, buttery popcorn, she tried to say, "This isn't for dogs, bud."

Afternoon would soon fade to evening, and she stood over the kitchen sink, looking out her back window as she ate another handful of popcorn. What was she going to do? Why hadn't Lawrence texted?

In the end, Roger's patience won out, and she gave him a single puff of popcorn. Then she pulled her hair up into a rough ponytail, leashed the pup, and stuffed a handful of dog treats in her pocket. "Let's go for a walk, boy," she told him, and he nearly pulled her to the ground in his enthusiasm to leave the house. Maybe he'd gotten a sugar rush already.

She'd reached the end of the block when a sleek, navy-as-midnight Mercedes-Benz rounded the corner at a crawl. A moment later, the driver braked hard, bringing the car to a stop. Maizee had stopped too, and her first thought was about what she was wearing.

Lawrence got out of the car before she could so much as release her hair from its hideous ponytail. "Hey," he said easily as if he saw her in such dire conditions every day. "You left work early?"

"You're just now finding out?" she asked. "I left at ten o'clock this morning."

Lawrence slowed in his approach toward her. "Why's that?"

Maizee glanced up and down the street, uncomfortable

out in the open now when she wasn't before. The addition of Lawrence to her sleepy neighborhood changed everything, and Maizee wasn't sure if she liked that or not.

He closed the distance between them and took one of her hands in his. "You look fantastic."

"I'm wearing a shirt that says 'Save the Clock Tower.'" She scoffed, ridiculous tears pressing up and behind her eyes.

"I like *Back to the Future,*" he said with a slow smile. "Why'd you leave early today?"

"Winthrop Porter arrived," she said, snapping the P's in his name. "And I freaked out. Didn't want to see him. Didn't want to think about what you two were talking about." She pressed her forehead to his breastbone, almost desperate to know what they'd talked about but too embarrassed to ask.

He stroked his free hand down the back of her head and took Roger's leash from her. "Let's walk, sweetheart."

Sweetheart.

Maizee didn't know what to do with the tenderness in his voice, but when he stepped, so did she. He went to his car first and turned off the ignition. "It'll be okay here, right?"

"It's not a high-crime neighborhood."

"I just meant here on the curb." He peered at her as if she'd revealed something crucial. "Oh, wow."

"What?"

Lawrence straightened and let Roger weave back and forth in front of them, something Maizee would've never done. The terrier was supposed to walk on her left side, not in front or behind her, but beside her. She didn't have the energy to say anything. So what if her dog developed bad habits? It wasn't like she walked him every day.

Lawrence's feet ate up half a block before he spoke again. "Does my money…bother you?"

"Bother me?"

"It changes how you view me."

"Well, uh, yeah. You're a billionaire. You own and operate a multi-billion dollar financial institution."

"And yet, I've been challenging myself to do things I've never done." He didn't look at her and Roger continued to do whatever he pleased.

"What does that have to do with anything?"

He took a deep breath. "It means that money doesn't make a person infallible."

"I know you're not perfect."

"Do you?" He stopped and looked at her, tugging Roger to let him know he needed to come back. "If you knew I was coming over tonight, what would you be wearing?"

Maizee stared at him. "Not this."

"Exactly." He fingered the hem of her T-shirt, which somehow sent chills through her whole body. "But I like this. I like seeing you be you."

Maizee thought about the heaping bucket of caramel corn on her kitchen counter and how she would've thrown it in the dishwasher last minute just to hide it from him. "I don't understand," she said.

Lawrence chuckled and lifted her knuckles to his lips. "I am not looking for the perfect woman. I'm looking for the perfect woman *for me.*"

She frowned, sifting through what he could possibly

mean by that. So she missed him leaning toward her until his mouth grazed hers. Then he kissed her like she was the perfect woman for him, and she forgot that she was wearing sweat pants and that her breath probably smelled and tasted like burnt, old popcorn kernels.

"Mm," he said, his mouth barely leaving hers. "You taste like sugar." He kissed her again, right there on the street for anyone to see.

"I like you, Maizee Phelps," he whispered next. "Just the way you are." He tucked her into his side, turned, and walked back toward her house.

Maizee went with him, because his kisses had turned her muscles to marshmallows, and she feared she might not be able to stand up by herself.

She wasn't sure she believed him. No man had ever liked her just the way she was. Winn had made that very clear.

TWELVE

LAWRENCE FOUND the source of the sugar sitting on Maizee's kitchen counter. "Holy lava rocks. What is this?" He picked up the movie theater bucket of popcorn, but it was covered in the most delectable looking caramel he'd ever seen.

"I always bring the leftovers home and make caramel corn," she said, as if every human being on Earth knew about this and did it.

But Lawrence continued to gaze that the concoction with wonder. "Why have I been throwing away my popcorn for forty-one years?"

Maizee finally laughed, and she scooped up a handful of the caramel corn. "Eat it. It's not bad."

"Not bad," Lawrence echoed, plucking a few pieces out of the bucket and putting them in his mouth. It was sweet and salty, soft and crunchy, everything he wanted in a late night snack. Or a five-thirty p.m. snack.

"This is amazing," he said, twisting toward Maizee to find her finger-combing out her hair. He wanted to tell her to stop, that he liked the messy look, the wisps of blonde hair spilling out, the way it exposed her neck.

He liked the funky T-shirt and the tight exercise pants. She seemed real, and he craved real after a day of dressed up, stuffy men, frustrating phone calls with his father, and negotiations on a deal that should've finalized by five o'clock.

Pushing out a breath, he asked, "Can we sit outside?"

"Rough day?" She went first and bypassed the picnic table where they'd eaten pizza and talked about the flower farm in the hills.

"Actually, yes." If he couldn't get her to talk, he'd do it. Opening up last time had helped, and maybe before he left tonight, he could figure out why she'd left in the morning, gone to a movie alone, and then made caramel corn.

She sat in one of two swings in an ancient swing set, the chains creaking with the addition of her weight. Lawrence joined her, but with some measure of trepidation squirreling through him. "I asked Winthrop to come meet with me, because his branch is…."

Lawrence wasn't quite sure how to classify it—and it wasn't really any of Maizee's business anyway. But he wanted to share his life with her, and his work was a big part of his life.

"Failing?" she supplied.

"You knew?"

"I know he struts around the place like he's you," she

said. "All while more and more people take their money and go somewhere else."

He pushed himself back with his toes. "That was all the meeting was about. He didn't mention you, and neither did I."

"How kind of him," she bit out. Lawrence looked at her. "He knows I transferred here, to this branch." Hurt passed through her eyes, and Lawrence wanted to gather it all into his arms and fling it into the ocean, where it would wash away and never bother her again.

She shook her head and looked away. "It doesn't matter. I'm not wasting any more of my time on Winthrop Porter."

Lawrence was glad to hear that, but he also heard the irritation and pain in her voice, and he knew without a doubt that she was not ready to fall in love again. He questioned why he'd allowed himself to fall so quickly, and again the idea that she was the perfect woman for him wouldn't leave his mind.

"Then my father called, and I answered it," he said, going on to detail the hour-long conversation about the Austin Exchange, and what angle Lawrence might play next. "But I don't play angles."

Maizee stalled herself in the swing until they were side-by-side, and she reached for his hand. "You don't play games, that's true." She sounded softer, more like herself. "So what happened?"

"Well, the acquisition didn't go through today," he said. "I'll have to get up early and get on the phone again." He swung back and forth with her. Back and forth. "I hate talking on the phone."

She squeezed his hand. "You're really good at it."

"How would you know?" he teased. "I always text you."

"You wrote an article about it once," she said. "In the company newsletter."

Lawrence had absolutely no recollection of that, but he didn't say so. The fact that Maizee knew that added another insight into why she'd placed him so high up on a pedestal. She'd known him first as the CEO, the owner, the boss.

So he'd just have to work at getting her to see him as Lawrence Gladstone, a regular man who happened to have a lot of money. But still a regular man, with fears and worries and dreams.

"So I think I'd like to try sea kayaking next," he said.

"Yeah?" She beamed at him.

"Yeah. But we can have the Coast Guard on speed dial, right?"

Maizee laughed, tipping her head back and revealing that lovely neck once more. But Lawrence didn't join her, because he really wasn't kidding. He'd call one of his SEAL buddies, just to let him know when they were going out and where they'd be.

He was cautious, that was all.

Oh, and he wanted to live to kiss Maizee again too.

They swung for a bit longer, and Maizee finally stood up. "You hungry?"

"Starving."

"Good, take me to dinner." She skipped ahead of him into the house, and by the time he entered through the back door, she was gone. He knew right where she was though:

changing her clothes, and freshening up her makeup, and putting on her jewelry.

Sure enough, she came down the hall ten minutes later looking like she was ready to attend her best friend's wedding. While Lawrence liked this sight of her too, the tight pants would've been fine.

"Do you like dressing up?" he asked as they left through the front door.

"Sometimes," she said, a guarded edge in her voice.

"What about just to go to a taco truck on the beach?" he asked. "Do you need heels for that?"

"I'm not wearing heels," she said. "My ankle still isn't at a hundred percent."

Lawrence exhaled, wishing he knew how to frame this conversation. He opened the passenger door for her and walked around the front, his mind churning. Behind the wheel, and driving down to the beach, he tried again. "I wouldn't have cared if you didn't change."

"Lawrence," she said, and he thought it might be one of the first times she'd said his name. He didn't like that it carried a warning undercurrent, but he pressed on anyway.

"I'm just wondering, Maizee. Why do you get all dolled up?"

"Is it wrong if I want to look my best in public?"

"Not if it's you who wants it."

She reached down to her feet for her purse and fiddled with it on her lap, finally pulling out a stick of gum. "I do."

"And I don't think so." He parked the car across the street from Manni's noting the long line. He'd forgotten about Manic Mondays, where the mahi mahi tacos were buy one get one free.

Didn't matter. He didn't have anywhere else to be. *With anyone else*, he thought, slipping a little further toward being in love with Maizee.

"Winn didn't—*Winthrop* liked it when I looked nice," she finally said, holding perfectly still in the passenger seat.

A slow anger began in Lawrence's gut. "He told you that?"

"He suggested the earrings I should wear with a certain sweater," she said, her voice robotic now. "He bought my shoes most of the time. He once pulled me into his office to say I'd worn the wrong pair with my skirt. He was…."

"A jerk," Lawrence said, quickly adding, "Sorry."

"No." She shook her head. "You're right. He was a jerk. I just didn't know it at the time. I was so desperate to please him."

Lawrence touched her arm, hoping to get her attention, get her to look at him. She swung her head toward him in slow motion, her beautiful blue eyes too watery for his liking. "You should get to be you." He leaned his head toward hers until their foreheads touched. "I like you just how you are."

"You keep saying that," she whispered. "And it makes me think you're insane." She half-laughed, half-sobbed, quickly leaning away from him and swiping at her eyes. "This is ridiculous. Let's go get a burrito." She got out of the car in a hurry after that, and Lawrence gave her a few seconds alone before he got out too.

He didn't want to push her too hard, push her too far

away. But he couldn't help linking his fingers through hers and saying, "Then I guess I'm insane."

She didn't answer, and Lawrence was smart enough to drop it at that point. But her confession and emotional display had only convinced him of one thing: He would show her and tell her he liked her how she was until she believed him, until she knew how wonderful she was—with or without makeup and earrings.

———

Lawrence couldn't get the deal on Austin Exchange closed during the next day. Or even the next week.

In fact, three weeks went by before their negotiations felt less than strained and sometimes downright hostile. At some point, Lawrence thought he'd lose the deal completely, and he couldn't imagine having to tell his father about that.

He threw out all his notes and made new ones. Talked to everyone he'd spoken with previously and dug up anyone new that he could. He spent most evenings with Maizee, but he was afraid he was poor company, especially because he showed up with food, they ate, and she made him something with a lot of chocolate in it.

He was comfortable with her, and she didn't seem to mind him crashing on her couch or in her backyard hammock and then baking for him while he went over sheets and sheets of numbers, re-read emails, or made late-night phone calls to contacts all over the US.

At the beginning of the fourth week, the tension in Lawrence's neck required an expensive massage therapist, but he'd hit a major breakthrough. Daniel Austin had taken his sweet time to review Lawrence's new proposal and had responded to his email with four words that made all of Lawrence's sleepless nights worth it.

When can we talk?

He whooped, right there in his office, his first thought to run downstairs and share this news with Maizee. He'd gotten very good at walking past her office with nothing more than a friendly wave, though if anyone at the branch had bothered to drive by her house, they'd find his Benz in the driveway almost every evening.

He quickly tapped out a response—*My schedule is wide open. I can call you anytime. Just let me know*—and practically ran down the stairs, swinging around to enter Maizee's office with a "You will not believe the—"

Email I just got died on his lips as he realized Maizee had customers in her office. "I'm so sorry." He backed out of the office, both hands up in a general display of *I apologize.*

He caught Maizee's eye, and she couldn't be more surprised than if he'd dropped to one knee and proposed.

His excitement built up inside him, and he couldn't stand to wait around in the lobby. So he strode out, his smile practically bursting off his face. He checked his email to see if Daniel had responded and found a bench just down from the bank that was drenched in shade.

He sat down, and said to the older woman there, "I just got a really great email."

She stared at him like he might be an alien invader and actually scooted down a little bit.

"I mean, you probably won't care, but it was a great email for me."

The woman got up and walked away, leaving Lawrence to check his phone again to see if Daniel had responded. Still nothing. But it was a glorious day in Getaway Bay, with an ocean breeze, and the sound of laughter and the ocean waves in the distance. If he walked down the road another block and turned south, he'd be able to see the beach, but he stayed right where he was in the shade.

About ten minutes later, Daniel still hadn't responded, but Lawrence's phone buzzed, indicating a text. *Where'd you go?*

From Maizee.

That manic smile came back, and Lawrence tapped on the phone icon to call her. Before the call could connect, another one came in.

Daniel.

Lawrence almost dropped his phone in his haste to end the call with Maizee and open the one with Daniel.

"Mister Austin," he said smoothly, glad the swooping in his stomach couldn't be conveyed through phone lines and across oceans.

"I liked your last proposal," Daniel said, no hello or formality in sight.

Thank goodness, Lawrence thought but didn't say. "What did you like about it?" he asked instead. His father had taught him that. *Listen more than you talk. Ask more than you answer. Be more offensive than defensive.*

"I think the price is finally right," he said. "But I'm not keen on point seven."

Lawrence had been through the proposal forward and backward. "The health insurance? Everyone on your team will be seamlessly integrated at Gladstone Financial."

"No, the severance insurance for me and my family."

Lawrence blinked. "It's very standard to offer the twelve months," he said. "And then it's up to you."

"That's the part I don't like."

Of course he didn't. But Lawrence was paying almost six hundred million dollars for a company worth five and a half, and he wasn't going to give Daniel Austin and his family unlimited health insurance until the day they died.

"I can offer eighteen months," Lawrence said. "But I'm afraid that's all."

The silence on the other end of the line unnerved him, and he almost blurted that he'd give Daniel whatever he wanted. But he held that tongue, like his father had taught him. Silence didn't always mean something bad. And he knew how to be silent too.

"My son has recently been diagnosed with juvenile diabetes," he said, his voice on the quiet end, almost like he'd moved the phone away from his mouth to speak.

"I'm very sorry to hear that." Lawrence's phone rumbled and beeped, the indication that another call was coming in. It was probably Maizee, and a hint of anxiety passed through him.

"My wife is worried about moving insurances so soon after the diagnosis," Daniel said.

Lawrence said nothing, hoping Daniel would have a solution to his own problem.

"I need four years," he said. "And I'm willing to take four million off the purchase price to get it."

Lawrence let another beat of silence go by, and then he said, "I can do that. I'll get my lawyer to draw up the changes."

"Thank you," Daniel said, and it wasn't hard to hear the relief in the man's voice. "You're a good man, Lawrence."

The call ended, and Lawrence stood next to the bench, feeling many things that didn't fully settle.

He'd done it. Negotiated one of the biggest deals in Gladstone Financial's history, and he'd helped someone too.

Instead of calling Maizee, he headed back to the bank, ready to celebrate with her face-to-face.

THIRTEEN

MAIZEE STOOD at the window in her office, watching cars ease down the street. She'd tried calling Lawrence back, but his line had gone to voice mail. He'd literally called her a moment before, but her phone hadn't even rung.

It did now, and she swiped open the call with, "Where did you go?"

"Nowhere," a female voice said, and Maizee whipped her phone away from her ear to see her sister's name on the screen.

"Oh, hey, Evie," she said. "I thought you were someone else."

"Who?" she asked, though she surely hadn't called to know that.

Maizee took a deep breath, her mind oscillating between telling her sister about Lawrence and keeping him secret just a little longer. But it had been weeks since they'd started seeing each other, and she did want to let everyone know that she'd moved on from Winn.

"Oh, just my boyfriend," she said, a happy hint in her voice. She expected Evie to shriek or ask a million questions.

She got silence.

She checked the phone again, but the call was still connected. As her sister started to talk, Maizee put the phone back to her ear.

"…been going on?" Evie finished.

"Oh, several weeks now."

"You left Lanai several weeks ago."

Maizee glanced over her shoulder, but no one loitered in her open doorway. Lawrence had not returned. She felt certain she'd know the moment he stepped foot in the build-ing. "He's my boss."

"Is he a better boss than Winn? Because that man is the worst." The venom in her sister's voice made Maizee feel better, actually.

"I think he's quite a bit better than Winn."

"You were always too good for him."

Yeah, well, now she had a boyfriend that was too good for her. She kept that thought to herself, though, because she was working on believing that he could like her as much as he claimed to.

"Thank you for saying so," she said, catching sight of a sharp dressed man striding down the street. Lawrence. She needed to wrap this conversation up quickly.

"Did you need something?" she asked her sister.

"Just calling to chat," she said. "Jules is so wrapped up in Johnny. It's Johnny and Jules, and Jules and Johnny, and…."

She let the words hang there, which clued Maizee into the fact that she had something important to say.

"And what?" She turned toward the door, watching for Lawrence. He would stop by, wouldn't he? Or would he walk up to his office without popping in? Seeing him burst through the door earlier had really put her heart in a shock, and she was just starting to feel more settled.

"I got a date with Tommy Pinnacle, and I need *help*."

So this wouldn't be a short conversation.

"Is he still going by Tommy?"

"Yes, and he's the *cutest*." Though her sister had just turned thirty, apparently *cutest* was still a word she could use when talking about boys. Of course, she was about to go out with a grown man named Tommy, so that was probably okay.

She also didn't get many dates, and Maizee wished she were there in Lanai to help her, especially with bubbly, always-had-a-date Jules on the prowl.

Lawrence's broad shoulders filled the doorway, his face one of beauty and grace and pure joy. She held up one finger, silently begging him to wait. Thankfully, he ducked into the office and closed the door.

He busied himself with closing all of her blinds while she said, "Evie, I would love to help you, but I just had a customer walk in. Can I call you at lunch?"

"Sure," her sister said, none the wiser that her "customer" was the man she hoped would kiss her until she couldn't breathe.

"Great. Talk soon." She hung up and flung her phone

onto the desk just as Lawrence finished with the last set of blinds.

He turned toward her, magnificent and radiant, and Maizee once again wondered why he liked her. "The Austin Exchange is ours." He laughed, the sound heartfelt and happy, and he grabbed onto her and twirled her in a circle. "I closed the deal."

"Good job," she said behind half a squeal, holding onto him as he steadied her on her feet. He gazed down at her, his smile so wide she thought she could get lost in it.

He kissed her, half-laughing so their mouths didn't quite match up. She giggled and leaned her forehead against his. "You've been working on that for weeks."

"Oh, did someone miss me?"

"Yes," she said, not trying to hide how she felt about him. She ran her hands down the front of his jacket, straightening it and enjoying the playfulness between them.

"I missed you too," he said, suddenly serious. He ran his fingers through her hair and this time when he leaned down to kiss her, it was the kind of kiss she always wanted.

She lost herself for a few moments, purely wrapped up in the taste and touch of him. Somewhere, far beyond her circle of conscious thought, she heard the noise from the lobby.

Which meant…someone had opened the door.

She jumped out of Lawrence's arms at the same time he turned.

"There you are," a man said, but Maizee couldn't see him around Lawrence. She knew that voice though….

"Winn?" dripped out of her mouth and she side-stepped to peer around Lawrence. Her whole face heated, and she wanted to crawl beneath her desk the way she had in grade school when they had earthquake drills.

He flicked a glance at her as if she wasn't worth his attention and then did a double-take. "Maizee?" The color left his face, and he looked back and forth between her and Lawrence.

"What are you doing here?" Lawrence practically barked, moving forward. He tossed over his shoulder, "I'll come back, Miss Phelps," and walked out, guiding Winn in front of him. And while all of Maizee's blinds were closed, she caught one last look of surprise on Winn's face before he was forced to turn and head up the stairs just outside her office.

She slumped into her chair, feeling weak and breathless and not only because Lawrence had stolen her heart.

Realization hit her, and she took several long moments to savor that she'd fallen in love with Lawrence Gladstone.

Then she muttered, "What a stupid thing to do, Maizee," and pulled her mouse closer to her so she could check her email. After all, he still wasn't ready to show their relationship to anyone.

So maybe this wasn't real to him. Maybe she really was just someone to keep him occupied in the evenings, though she'd never felt like that before.

Worry needled her, but she managed to go through her emails and read through two online applications before finding the right percentage rate and approving the loans. She kept her blinds closed and her door open, but she didn't see Lawrence or Winn leave.

Her skin itched, and just when she was going to go marching upstairs and find out what in the world Winn was doing on the island *again,* she heard footsteps coming down. A loud voice.

She got up from her desk and hurried around it, thanking the stars that her ankle had healed completely. She arrived at her door at the same time Winn hit the ground floor. "You're dating *him* now?" He practically threw a punch toward the steps, where Lawrence was hurrying down.

Maizee had no idea what to say. Winn's loud shout had drawn the attention of nearly everyone in the bank, and she felt the weight of all the eyes in the building.

Winn leaned closer, his eyes angry and the scent of him so familiar. "Did I mean nothing to you?"

She scoffed, her own fury shooting to the top of her head. "Are you serious? You broke up with me, remember?"

"Not so you could run off to a bigger island and date your next boss."

"Would you stop it?" Lawrence said, his face flushed.

"You know he's ruthless, right?" Winn said next. "Rigid. No flexibility at all. No compassion." He glared at Lawrence. "I can't believe...." Winn shook his head. "I just can't." He spun and stormed off, leaving so much awkwardness in his wake that Maizee was having a hard time breathing.

Winn left the bank, and Lawrence sprang into action. "All right, everyone. Back to work." He glanced at Maizee, said nothing, and went right back upstairs as if he didn't need to clarify anything else.

She glanced around the bank, catching the surprise on Polly's face and the displeasure on Willie's. Suddenly her head was too heavy to keep up, and she ducked, turned, and scampered back into her office.

———

Maizee let forty-eight hours go by before she stood in front of the mirror and told herself, "Call him. You didn't do anything wrong."

If anything, Lawrence was the one who needed to apologize. It wasn't against the company policy to date a co-worker, and they were two consenting adults. But she'd been hiding out in her office for long enough, and now the branch manager had asked her for a meeting the following morning.

Maybe she should just quit. She'd thought about it more than once, especially in the past couple of days, but the thought scared her still. She couldn't believe she was almost forty years old and still didn't have a life that made sense.

And she didn't call Lawrence that night. Or in the morning. She met with Willie McMahon in her best skirt suit, determined to leave Gladstone Financial with her head held high, no matter what.

"This has nothing to do with Mister Gladstone," Will said to start the meeting. He put on a pair of reading glasses and picked up a piece of paper. "We've had a complaint."

Everything in her body turned to ice. "What?" She wanted to see what was on the paper but she could've been just as happy tearing it up. "I have done a great job here." And she would defend that to the death.

"Not that kind of complaint." He laid the paper aside, a measure of softness entering his expression.

Maizee frowned, her heart beating out a cadence in her chest that couldn't be maintained for much longer. "I'm sorry. What?"

"One of the employees feels uncomfortable with your relationship with Mister Gladstone. She had, uh." He cleared his throat. "Put in for the loan officer job, and claims you got it unfairly."

"That's not true. I transferred from the Lanai branch. I didn't even know Lawrence—" She inhaled sharply. "I did not even know Mister Gladstone before coming here."

"Nevertheless, I need—"

The door opened, interrupting him, and Lawrence stood there. "Will," he said, taking in the scene before him. "Maizee?"

"Come in, Lawrence." Will gestured him in with flapping hands and a big sigh. "I suppose I can get both of your statements at the same time."

Lawrence entered the office and took a seat beside Maizee. She hadn't seen him in days, and she wanted to rage at him. Demand to know why he'd gone silent and left this all on her.

"Statement?" she squeaked out.

"About your relationship." Will slid two papers toward them, one for each of them.

Maizee stared at it in horror. Things were spiraling rapidly out of control.

"Relationship?" Lawrence picked up the paper. "I'm not writing any statement."

Maizee turned her head and looked at him, everything happening in slow motion. "Why not?"

Lawrence barely looked at her. "I own the company."

"Which is why it could be very bad for you," Willie said, probably in the gentlest voice he could muster.

Lawrence made a noise of exasperation, and Maizee made a quick decision. She jumped to her feet. "I'm not making a statement either. At least not a written one. I met Lawrence on the trail up to the Umauma Falls. Of course I knew who he was. I've worked for this company for almost two decades, and he sends a newsletter on the fifteenth of every month, even if it's a weekend or a holiday."

Her chest burned for lack of oxygen, and she wondered what she'd say next.

"I didn't do anything wrong. I didn't use any relationship to get my job. I transferred from the Lanai branch." She pushed out her breath, wishing Lawrence would leap to his feet and corroborate everything she'd said.

He sat there. Sat there and did nothing.

"And you know what?" She glared at him and then Will McMahon. "I quit." She turned, ignoring Lawrence's call of "Maizee, come on. You can't quit," and left the office. Left the bank.

Simply walked out and left.

FOURTEEN

LAWRENCE THOUGHT GIVING Maizee some space was a good thing. It had always worked in the past. But watching her walk out of Will's office, the bank, and his life, he realized that he was dead wrong.

He should've called her and then gone to her house the very night Winn had showed up and said such horrible things about him. He knew how Maizee's mind worked, and she probably hadn't slept more than a few hours each night as she went round and round everything.

"I really need a statement," Will said.

"Why?" Lawrence barked. "We both know Winthrop Porter made that complaint, not anyone here at this branch, and that he's just looking to get me and this company in trouble."

Lawrence had really tried with the man, but he wasn't any good at his job and the remediation hadn't gone well. Lawrence supposed he was ruthless when it came to dealing with Winn, but meetings and checks and the probation period were the same things he would've done with any employee at Gladstone.

Winn had not responded well, and Lawrence didn't want to work today. He stood, left Will sitting in his office with two blank papers, and left the office. He wanted to rush over to Maizee's house, but he suspected she wouldn't go there.

No, she'd go somewhere she loved best, where she could think. Maybe the beach. Maybe a waterfall. Maybe out in the middle of nowhere with a sack lunch and a bottle of sunscreen.

He pulled out his phone and called her, silently praying that she'd answer. Relief hit him hard in the gut when the phone stopped ringing after only two *bleeps!*

"Lawrence," she said, her voice soft and even and absolutely wonderful in his ears. "I don't want to talk to you right now. Please."

"I'm sorry," he said.

"Yeah? About what?"

He wasn't sure, and he apparently took too long to say, because she said, "Call me back when you figure it out." The line went dead, and Lawrence stared at the screen as it went back to his homepage.

"Is that it?" he asked the air around him. "Did she just break up with me?"

"Do you always talk to yourself?"

He glanced over at the same woman sitting on the bench where she'd been the last time he was here, telling her about his great email. That seemed like it had happened such a long time ago, not just three days.

That had been one of the highest moments of his life. And this, standing here on the sidewalk without Maizee and with Winn's ridiculous claim, felt like one of the lowest.

"Not always," he said, adjusting his jacket. He didn't know where to go next, so he simply walked. He ignored the beach to his right and continued around the bend in the road, Sweet Breeze coming into view up ahead.

His Nine-0 Club. They'd know what to do. Well, at least about the false claim by his former branch manager in Lanai. At least Will was a decent manager, and he'd agreed to drag his feet on it before escalating it up the chain of command. And there was no way Lawrence's father could find out.

His stride lengthened, and he reached Sweet Breeze a few minutes later. "Mister Gladstone," one of the security guards said as he walked in. "Welcome."

"Hey, Maxim," he said, taking a minute to shake the man's hand.

"Your tip about the clothing stock was right on," Maxim said.

"Hmm," he said, not wanting to give away that he knew the owners personally and that they'd discussed their launch during one of their Club meetings. "Is Fisher in?"

"Owen would know."

Lawrence nodded and headed over to the registration desk. He stepped to the right, toward the concierge, who usually knew if Owen was in or out and where he might be if he was gone.

"Hey, Jean," Lawrence said with a quick smile. "Have you seen Owen?"

The woman tucked her dark hair and batted her

eyelashes at him. Lawrence had never paid much attention to her, but all of a sudden he realized she'd been flirting with him for months. He felt a twinge of guilt about not noticing and looked away.

"He's in his office," she said. "I think Fisher's there too."

"Great." He tapped twice on the counter and moved down the hallway toward the offices of his friends. The door to Owen's office was open, and voices filtered into the hall. Lawrence stalled. Sure, he was friends with Fisher and Owen, but he wouldn't call them besties. He'd always related more to Ira, but he was on a cruise with Gabi, probably getting engaged as the sun set into the ocean.

Lawrence thought of the last time he'd been on a boat, the sun sinking into the ocean. Maizee's favorite time of the day, she'd said. And how wonderful had it felt to hold her, his heart thumping in his chest, telling him that it was scared but it didn't want to stop.

So Lawrence continued on into the office, a little on the scared side but unable to keep holding himself back.

He knocked on the door and said, "Hey," to get their attention. Owen sat at his desk, seemingly working, while Fisher relaxed in a chair opposite of him. He jumped to his feet when he saw Lawrence.

"Hey." Surprise filled his face and the word, but he shook Lawrence's hand. "What brings you by?"

Owen likewise stopped working, his face also full of curiosity. "Water?" he asked.

"I'm okay," Lawrence said, immediately thirsty. He sat in another chair, glad when Fisher sat too. "Actually, I will take some water."

Owen bent and pulled a bottle of water out from underneath his desk. He obviously had a little fridge down there, because the water was cold as it slid down Lawrence's throat.

"I need some advice," he said, capping his bottle again.

"Marshall will be here in a few minutes," Fisher said. "Do you want to wait?"

"I think he can get caught up." Lawrence wiped his hand down his face. "My branch manager in Lanai has been on probation for several weeks. His ex-fiancée is now the loan manager at the branch here, having moved after they broke up." He hesitated and pulled at his collar.

"Uh, when we met, we sort of hit it off and have been seeing each other since she got here."

Fisher's face broke into a grin. "Lawrence. I didn't know you dated."

"No wonder we haven't seen him at meetings recently," Marshall said from his position in the doorway.

Lawrence whipped his head toward him. "How long have you been standing there?"

"Long enough to hear you have a girlfriend."

"Had," Lawrence said. "Maybe. I don't know."

"I'm sure he didn't come here for dating advice." Marshall accepted the bottle of water Owen handed to him and sat on the black leather couch against the wall.

Lawrence gave himself a mental shake. "No, I'm not. That branch manager found out that Maizee and I were dating, and he's filed a complaint with the company. It's anonymous, but I know it's him."

"What kind of claim?" Owen asked.

"He made it sound like it came from a female at the branch here, and that Maizee got the promotion because of our relationship."

"True or not?" Marshall asked, always wanting the facts before saying much of anything.

"Completely untrue," Lawrence said. "She transferred here from the Lanai branch, because Bennie retired. In fact, we hadn't had a loan officer for about three weeks before her transfer request came in. Of course Will took it."

"So there's a third party," Fisher said. "Who's Will?"

"My Getaway Bay branch manager."

"So he would know that you didn't have anything to do with the job appointment."

"Of course. But we have protocols."

"Follow them," Owen said.

"He wanted a statement." Lawrence rolled his eyes, realizing how stupid some of the policies at Gladstone Financial were.

"Better give it then," Fisher said. "Tell your side of the story. Say what you just told us so it's put on someone else."

He nodded, realizing he should've filled out the form. "Maizee quit. I'm worried that will imply she was guilty."

Fisher and Owen exchanged a look, but Lawrence couldn't tell if it was a good one or a bad one. "It could," Owen said. "But we lose people all the time. It's best to follow the procedures."

"At the very least, it protects you," Fisher said.

Lawrence nodded, and the conversation turned to something else. Something light. The men went down the hall to the bistro off the lobby for lunch, and Lawrence joined them.

He had missed several of the last Nine-0 Club meetings, preferring to spend his free time with Maizee, and he missed his friends.

He thought through the happenings of the last few days, through everything that had brought him to be sitting here in the middle of the day. He'd been quiet when he should've said something. He'd given her space when she didn't want or need it.

He'd laid low, waiting for her to come to him. He should've been the one to go to her, and he slid to the end of the bench. "I have to go."

"Go where?" Fisher asked.

"To talk to Maizee." He reached into back pocket and withdrew his wallet. After tossing some cash on the table for his part of the meal, he said, "I've got to be brave." He wasn't sure if he was telling his friends or himself. He just knew he'd figured out at least one thing he needed to apologize for, and he wanted to find Maizee as soon as possible to do that.

He pulled his phone out as soon as he hit the great outdoors, but Maizee's phone just rang and rang and rang. Frustrated, he walked faster.

FIFTEEN

MAIZEE DIPPED the oar into the water over and over, the waves quite calm today. Or maybe the waves coming into Getaway Bay were always like this. The shoreline of Lanai was choppier for sure, requiring more attention. But here, she could stroke and think, think and stroke.

She wasn't sure if she liked it or not.

She wasn't sure of a lot of things at the moment. Thus, sea kayaking in the middle of the day, after quitting her job.

Her chest squeezed. She could not believe she'd quit her job. Given up her retirement. Everything she'd worked for nineteen years at Gladstone Financial. One more year and she could've qualified for a decent pension, a great sever-ance health insurance package.

She wanted to cry, but there were no tears. She wanted to yell, but her voice remained silent.

She put the oar in the water and pulled, over and over and over. Lawrence should be here with her, as she'd promised him several times to teach him how to sea kayak. Not that there was anything hard about it. She sat in a kayak and rowed around the bay. She'd been around the tip of land between the two bays, and she now faced the huge, twenty-eight story building in Getaway Bay.

Sweet Breeze Resort and Spa. She'd gone to many beach yoga classes on the sand there, and she'd seen Lawrence go inside the hotel once. He was probably friends with the owner of the hotel, both of them being billionaires and all.

She'd even gotten the instructor's number, especially once Tawny found out Maizee was dating Lawrence, who of course, she'd said her husband was friends with. So Tawny's husband was probably a billionaire too.

A bitterness filled her mouth. She hadn't exactly broken up with Lawrence, but they certainly weren't on speaking terms. She wanted to paddle up to shore, leave her kayak, and go see if he was at the hotel. Be brave and face him. Tell him she loved him, but he'd hurt her when he'd basically ignored her for two days and kept his mouth shut about their relationship to a bank full of employees that he managed.

See what he'd do then.

Instead, she rowed hard on the right, turning away from the beach and facing the open ocean. The sunlight glinted off the crests of the waves in bright, white sparkles that hurt her eyes, even through her sunglasses.

The waves pushed and pulled her, as she let the oar rest across the kayak. She felt just as adrift, willing to go in whatever direction the greatest force was taking her.

But she couldn't stay out in the kayak forever. So she

went back to East Bay where she'd parked and headed home after many hours of sun. Roger greeted her at the door, somehow knowing she'd gone kayaking without him.

"Sorry, bud," she said, all the energy she had to give to the dog. She showered, scooped the pup into her arms, and took him outside to the hammock. She laid in it with Roger, wishing her memories weren't full of Lawrence in this yard and this hammock.

She didn't even have a girlfriend to call and commiserate with. Yes, she'd seen Kara at the coffee shop every single morning, but they hadn't hung out much. Lawrence came over all the time, and Maizee hadn't minded.

She did now, and she wondered if she just needed some time to be herself. She hadn't been alone in years, and she wasn't sure she even knew how to be alone.

"Maizee?"

She sat straight up, sure she hadn't heard Lawrence's voice. She'd started to doze, and maybe she'd dreamt it.

But no, he definitely seemed to be walking toward her, slowing with every step. "Hey," he finally said, stopping a healthy distance away.

Maizee just stared at him.

"You said I could call when I figured out what I needed to apologize for."

"I didn't mean a house call." She hadn't done her hair or put on makeup after her shower. All at once, she didn't care. This was who she was, and Lawrence had always said he liked her just the way she was.

"I've called you a few times," he said.

"I was out on the ocean and haven't checked my phone." She wasn't even sure where it was at the moment.

He took another step forward and then fell back. "I should've defended our relationship," he said. "I'm sorry I didn't say anything."

All at once, Maizee felt like crying.

"We do need to fill out the statements Will wants us to," he said next, which made Maizee's emotions dry right up. "And I don't think you should quit. It makes you look guilty."

So he'd come to take care of business, not to take care of her. But she nodded, because maybe if she didn't have to quit, she could put in one more year and then take her retirement.

Problem was, she couldn't imagine going back to that bank tomorrow, let alone for another twelve months.

Maybe she could transfer again....

She pushed the idea out of her mind. She couldn't keep running from her problems, because *she* was the problem, and she couldn't run and hide from herself.

"Thank you," she said, wishing she wasn't in a hammock. She hated trying to get out of a hammock, especially in front of a handsome man she really wanted to be with.

"So you'll come back tomorrow?"

She nodded and extended her hand toward him. "Help me up, okay?"

He dashed forward and put his hand in hers, and her skin sizzled with heat and electricity still. "Dinner?" he asked, keeping her hand in his.

"Yes," she said. "I need dinner."

———

Maizee returned to the Getaway Bay branch of Gladstone Financial the next day, polished and professional and perfectly put together. She wanted to walk in with a makeup-less face and wearing a pair of jeans, but she simply couldn't do it. She was programmed to wear skirts and heels and dangly earrings. She actually liked doing so.

She ignored the looks from her co-workers, stopped by Will's office to pick up the paper she needed to fill out, and clicked her way over to her own office. She closed the door behind her, something she hadn't done very often in the several weeks she'd been there.

Working through the morning, she managed to get several things done that she should've accomplished yester-day. She took a lunch outside of the office, enjoying the autumn sun and the cool breeze.

The whole hour passed, and she stopped by a grilled cheese food truck for something to eat, and then a shaved ice truck with a pretty red-headed woman handing out the treats. When she returned to the bank, everything was back to normal.

Well, as normal as things could be when Lawrence wasn't in the building. She wondered where he was that day, but he hadn't texted her and she wasn't going to initiate the conversation. She had work to do, and she was going to do it.

That evening, she rode her bike along the coastal highway, all the way out to the ranch, where she ordered strawberry lemonade and a burger. Then she biked back, barely making it before darkness consumed the island.

She almost rear-ended a midnight-blue Benz.

"Where'd you go?" Lawrence asked from the front steps.

"Riding," she said.

He smiled at her warmly, but Maizee felt like something between them had shifted. And it had. She'd shifted. She'd changed.

"Lawrence," she said. "I think I need to take a page out of your book, and be brave."

"All right," he said.

"I need some time."

"Time?"

"Alone."

He looked like she'd punched him in the throat. "I—I—"

"Maybe I just need...." She sighed and looked away. "I don't know what I need, but I do know I need to figure it out. By myself."

Lawrence pocketed his hands. "So that's it."

"For now."

"I don't even know what that means."

"It means maybe I had just ended one relationship with my boss when I started another one, with an even bigger boss." Maizee didn't know what she was saying. "And I don't want to hurt you, and—"

"You haven't hurt me."

"Oh, well, good."

"Good." He fished his keys out of his pocket. "So I need to go."

"Of course." She walked her bike past his car as he got behind the wheel. The car roared to life in a way she'd never heard before, and he practically shot out of her driveway, obviously never looking back.

Maizee stared into the darkness at his fading taillights, wondering when things between them had gone off the rails, and if she'd ever be able to get them back on track.

————

The plane touched down on the island of Lanai, and a relief spread through her like a warm blanket covering her internal organs. Her mom would be waiting to pick her up, and they were going to lunch before heading back to the house, where Evie would be waiting for Maizee to help her get ready for her date with Tommy.

Maizee leaned her head against the thick airplane window, mourning the part of her heart that she'd left behind in Getaway Bay. Lanai would always feel like home, but she had enjoyed her time on the Big Island of Hawaii.

She wondered how much of that was due to Lawrence, though. She'd met him on the third day she'd been in Getaway Bay, and they'd spent so much time together since. She tried to put him out of her mind, but he wouldn't seem to go.

He did have a stubborn streak. And while she'd never been in his office, she knew he was brilliant and hard-working. She'd seen the exhaustion on his face in the evenings, listened to him talk about the Austin Exchange and the deal he was trying to work for a few minutes before he dragged himself back to his penthouse.

So he knew how to work. Knew how to run a huge, global financial company. But he didn't know how to explore the island, or sea kayak by himself. Maizee found those simple things ironic, and a smile touched her lips as the last of the passengers deplaned. She finally stood and collected her bag from the overhead compartment.

She smiled at the flight attendants, thanked the pilots, and dragged her carryon down the ramp to the cement. Once inside the airport, she stopped in the bathroom and steeled herself to see her mother for the first time in a few months.

She didn't want to cry, but she felt dangerously close to it already. Sure enough, when she caught sight of her mother's beautiful, brassy, blonde hair, tears pricked her eyes. "Mom," she called, and their eyes met.

Maizee hugged her, so glad she'd always have the comfort in these arms. "Hey, Mom."

"It's so nice of you to come help Evie," she said, stepping back and holding onto Maizee's shoulders. "Jules has been kind of a nightmare already, and the wedding isn't until next summer."

Maizee nodded. "She's always been high-maintenance."

Her mom laughed and reached for Maizee's bag. "Well, we all have, haven't we? I mean, you love jewelry and makeup. Evie loves headbands and anything that sparkles. And Jules is just the worst. She loves lipsticks and glitter and tight dresses. And flowers and water fountains." She started for the exit. "I keep telling her we can just have the wedding in our yard, but that doesn't seem good enough for her. Did you know she's hired and fired three wedding planners already?"

Maizee could actually believe that, and while she wanted to see her sisters again, she was glad she was in Lanai just for the weekend. "There's a great wedding planning place in Getaway Bay," she said. "Or so I've heard."

"Oh? Be sure to tell Jules about it." Her mom took a few steps and added, "She's not listening to anything I say anymore."

"She's only been engaged a few weeks," Maizee said.

"Like I said, bridezilla." Her mom threw a small smile over her shoulder, but Maizee heard the hurt beneath her mother's words. Jules would be the first of the sisters to be married, and her mother had probably been looking forward to the weddings of her kids for a long time. After all, she loved fine china and perfectly placed centerpieces and entertaining more than anyone Maizee knew.

She kept the conversation away from Jules during lunch, instead deciding to say, "So I met a man in Getaway Bay."

Her mother's fork stopped halfway to her mouth. "You did?"

Maizee nodded and tucked her hair behind her ear. "He's the owner of Gladstone Financial. We hit it off. Instant fireworks. He's so handsome." She half-laughed and half-sobbed as tears made another appearance.

"Oh, honey." After putting down her utensil, her mom covered Maizee's hand with both of hers. "It's over already?"

Maizee sniffed. "I mean, maybe. I don't know. I don't

know how to be…alone, Mom. I was with Winn for so long, and I met Lawrence almost as soon as I got to the island. I hadn't even started work yet."

"You know how to be alone," her mom said, picking up her fork again and stabbing at her chicken salad.

"Not really," Maizee said. "I dated Chad for four years before that ended. About a month later, I started dating Perry."

"Now, he was a disaster."

A laugh exploded out of Maizee's mouth, because she could only agree. "Yes, he was." But the truth was, she'd started dating Lynn after that, and then Michael, and then Homer. Some of them were flings, men she spent summers with hiking and laughing and flirting. Sometimes kissing. Sometimes making a real relationship for a few months. Maybe six or nine.

But none had been as long as the one with Winn, and she'd only ever worn one engagement ring. So no matter what her mother said, Maizee actually just did not know how to be alone.

After lunch, they drove to her childhood home, where Evie sat on the front steps, her head bent over her phone. She glanced up when their mom turned into the driveway, and she met Maizee with a smile, a squeal, and a squeeze.

"I'm so glad you're here," Evie said, linking her arm through Maizee's. "My hair needs serious help."

"It's fine," Maizee said. She'd always been a bit envious of Evie's cornsilk hair, and she ran her fingers through it as she said, "I'll get this curled right up. Tommy won't be able to keep his hands to himself."

SIXTEEN

LAWRENCE SAT ON THE BEACH, a bottle of diet Dr. Pepper in his hand that was half-empty and almost too warm to swallow. He hated the beach. Well, he liked the look of it. The smell of the ocean. The beautiful horizon line.

But he didn't like sand between his toes, or the smell of sunscreen, or wearing a hat for long periods of time. It was too windy today for an umbrella, and Lawrence didn't own one anyway. He rarely sat on the beach, because he didn't have the time nor inclination to do so.

But the wives of some of the other billionaires in the Nine-0 Club had some sort of women's club that literally sat on the beach for hours on end, chatting. Families came to the beach everyday. Heck, people paid good money to come to Getaway Bay and the beaches here to vacation. Relax.

But Lawrence did not feel relaxed. He hadn't since Maizee had told him she needed some time to figure out how to be alone.

He'd been alone for a long time, and it wasn't that great. Like, right now, sitting there in the sun, in the sand, listening to the surf, and he wasn't any happier than he would've been with her in her hammock. Or behind his desk, reading a report or researching a company and if he should invest in it.

The next day, he went sailing alone, about the bravest thing he knew how to do. He went to work, but he didn't come face-to-face with Maizee. She'd either kept track of his arrival and departure times so she could schedule her trips to the restroom or over to Polly's desk or out to lunch.

He wondered what she was doing on weekends, and if he might run into her if he decided to go hiking or biking or kayaking. Parasailing. Surfing. Ziplining. He could do all of it right here on Getaway Bay.

He'd started with the hike to Umauma Falls, but he'd never finished it. So after a few weekends sitting on his couch and watching four movies a day, he put on his hiking boots, filled a backpack with food, and even checked the weather before he left the penthouse.

The hike up the trail wasn't that hard though Lawrence wasn't exactly an athlete. He did climb a lot of stairs every day and the hike up to the falls wasn't much harder than that. The trees were still in bloom though October had arrived, and the air held a nice crispness this early in the morning.

He'd half-hoped he'd run into Maizee on this trail, but at the same time, he didn't want to see her quite yet. She'd said she needed time to be alone, and he wanted to give her that.

Her words *for now* circled in his head, giving him hope

no matter how long the day was or how hopeless he felt. And so it was those words which propelled him up the trail to the falls, where a handful of other people had already arrived.

He found a rock to sit on to guzzle a bottle of water, and he pulled a couple of granola bars out of his pack. The falls made a wonderful roaring noise, and Lawrence felt a rush of pride for having hiked a couple of miles in the wilderness to this spot.

He'd done it. He'd done it without Maizee, and it did feel amazing to check something off his list that he'd been wanting to do for a while.

So it was that the next weekend found him standing on the dock, wearing a life jacket, and listening to a boy no older than sixteen talk about currents and riptides, wakes and waves, and how to navigate in the sea kayak.

While Lawrence had wanted to get these instructions from Maizee and follow her blonde head out into the ocean, she wasn't around. He wondered what she was doing that morning, and if there was any possible way five weeks was long enough for her to figure anything out.

The wind snaked down his collar no matter how he tried to flip it up, but his oar moved through the water easily as he propelled himself out with the other people in the group. The tour guide pointed out landmarks along the shore, and even the form of a sea lion in the water.

Once again, Lawrence was reminded of Maizee and how much she would love to be that sixteen-year-old boy, giving sea kayaking lessons and then island shore tours.

When he got back to land, he decided to do one more

brave thing that morning. He pulled out his phone and texted her.

Just went sea kayaking. You were right. It was amazing!

He read the words over and over and decided they were fine. He'd gone sea kayaking and had fun. They'd talked about it a lot, and he wanted to tell her. So he tapped the arrow on the screen to send the message, hoping with everything in him that she'd respond.

When a few seconds passed and she didn't, he quickly tapped out *They have tour guides who teach people about it and take them out. You should totally do that.*

He wasn't sure if she would resent him saying that, but she had told him that she'd like to be a tour guide, and she loved sea kayaking. It seemed like a match made in heaven —just like he'd thought the two of them were.

He pulled in a breath when he realized that he'd fallen in love with Maizee Phelps.

When had that happened?

Lawrence turned in a circle like the answer would be written right there on the dock somewhere. A couple who'd been in his group went by, smiles on their faces. "See, I told you you'd like it," the man said to the woman. "And you didn't die."

They laughed together, and Lawrence wished Maizee stood next to him so they could joke and laugh too. His hand felt so empty, and the great experience he'd just had kayaking felt a little more hollow than it had a moment ago.

Then his phone buzzed, which was like a jolt of electricity straight to his heart. He almost didn't dare check who'd messaged him—after all, he received dozens of calls, texts, and emails every day, weekend or not—in case it wasn't Maizee.

But he was trying to be brave—wasn't that why he'd hiked to the falls and buckled himself into a kayak?—so he lifted the phone so he could check it.

Good for you!

From Maizee. That was it. Nothing more. Nothing about the tour guide.

Didn't matter. She'd responded, and happiness spread through Lawrence with the speed of the subway. Before, he had two words, and now he had three.

He tucked his phone back in his pocket and headed down the pier, thinking tacos sounded like a mighty fine lunch after a morning of sea kayaking and texting with his non-girlfriend.

———

"It's been two months," Jason said as he stuck the menu back in the holder on the table. He looked at Lawrence. "And you haven't spoken to her?"

"We've texted a little," Lawrence said, which wasn't a complete lie. It wasn't exactly true either, but he had messaged her and she had responded.

Jason ordered the pork nachos and the doughnut holes, got up and selected his club, and stepped over to the green. Lexie ordered colas and a BLT before the waiter turned to Lawrence. He got his drink as well as the poached eggs with ham before meeting Lexie's eyes.

"I'm sorry about Maizee," Lexie said.

"Me too," Lawrence said, an idea occurring to him. "You guys…I mean, you didn't get together right away."

Jason turned, this conversation obviously better than trying to hit a golf ball into a target. "No, we didn't," he said. "Lexie wouldn't allow it." He grinned at her and returned to the table, leaning down to kiss her along the forehead.

"That's not true," Lexie said. "There were issues."

"Every couple has them," Jason said. "She'll come back to you."

"Maybe." Lawrence didn't know what else to do. It had been eight weeks since Maizee had said she needed time to be alone. The holidays were approaching, and Lawrence had spent plenty of them by himself and he didn't want to do it again.

"You really like her?" Jason asked.

"Obviously," Lexie said. "I mean, look at him."

"Look at me?" Lawrence watched his friends. "What do I look like?"

"Like you're in love with her," Lexie said. "Which is fine, Lawrence. People fall in love. You don't need to be embarrassed about it."

"I'm not embarrassed about it."

"Does she know?" Jason asked.

Lawrence shook his head. "No, I didn't know until a couple of weeks ago." He pushed out his breath, glad when the food arrived and the conversation stalled. He cleared his throat. "But the case at work was settled. Dismissed, actually. Closed."

"That's great." Lexie smiled at him.

Lawrence nodded and said, "Yeah, it is. The branch

manager in Lanai has been replaced, and the committee ruled that neither Maizee nor I did anything wrong. So that's good."

"Really good," Jason agreed. "Look, man, you've just got to maybe go after what you want. You know? If you love this woman, go tell her."

"What if it drives her away?" He looked to Lexie for the answer, because while she had a good head for money and finance too, she was also a woman and would likely speak from the heart.

"No woman I know minds when a handsome man shows up and says he loves her." Lexie gave him an encouraging smile.

"You think he's handsome?" Jason asked.

"Oh, come on." Lexie laughed. "Look at him. He's drop-dead *gorgeous*. Any woman with even one eye would drool over him."

Lawrence gaped at Lexie. "I asked you out once. You said no."

Lexie shrugged, a smile all the way up in her eyes. "I didn't think you were my type."

"A drop-dead gorgeous man isn't your type?" Jason asked, his voice straying up into a different octave.

Lawrence laughed at the teasing glint in Lexie's eyes. "Oh, come on, man. I knew why she rejected me. She was already in love with someone else."

"Who?" they asked together, looking at one another.

"Duh," Lawrence said, rolling his eyes and picking up his fork to start in on the eggs.

"It was me, right?" Jason asked, chuckling.

"Duh," Lexie said before kissing him, and Lawrence usually didn't mind when they showed how much they loved each other in front of him. But this time, all it did was remind him of how lonely he was. How empty his life had been these last eight weeks, though he'd attempted to fill it with adventures and anything but indoor activities.

And how all he had was a giant penthouse apartment to go home to.

SEVENTEEN

MAIZEE HAD WORKED out with Willie to work from home three days a week. He opened her office in the morning as if she were there, but she handled all the online support now, as well as any loans that came in digitally. Polly set up appointments for her when she was in the physical building, and she made sure her door was closed during the times when Lawrence arrived or left.

Once or twice, he left in the middle of the day while she was in her office, and she'd rush to the bathroom or stare at the computer screen intently as if she were solving the hardest puzzle on earth.

He'd never come in, and he'd only texted one time. She'd responded, hoping he'd continue, tell her about the kayaking and what he'd seen. But he'd fallen into silence again, and Maizee didn't know how to break it.

She looked at her phone, wishing it would brighten with his name and picture on the screen. Roger shifted from his position on her feet, finally getting up and trotting over to the back door.

Maizee heaved herself out of the chair at the dining room table and let the dog out, standing there and inhaling the fresh air for a few minutes. Roger had come back in a while ago, and Maizee had work to do. She should go back in and do it.

She honestly wasn't sure she could do it for another few hours. And the thought of doing it for another year? A sigh leaked from her chest, and she turned back to the kitchen table, which she'd set up as a home office.

"Gotta keep doing it," she said as she sat down in front of her laptop. "One more year." She couldn't give up nineteen years of retirement savings and all the time she had already put in just because things were hard right now.

So she went through the loans, the emails, the customer service surveys. She filed everything the way she'd been told, and she sent her daily report to Willie.

He texted back with, *Great job, Maizee. You're the best.*

He had been highly complimentary of her work since the case had been opened, and Maizee was glad everything had been settled. Winn no longer worked for Gladstone Financial, as he'd had enough years at the company to retire and move on.

Her phone chimed again, this time with Evie's name on the screen. *Tommy and I are going out again tonight. Fourth date. Do you think it's too early to kiss him?*

Absolutely not, Maizee texted back. *Did he like your haircut?*

I think so? Evie said. *He grinned and ran his hand around the* back of my neck. *I actually thought he'd kiss me then, but he didn't. #sigh*

Definitely kiss him tonight, Maizee said. *And if he doesn't, just ask him when he's going to so you can stop worrying about it.*

Does that work?

In Maizee's experience, asking a man when he was going to kiss her *always* led to a kiss, usually only a few minutes later. Definitely that same day. So she texted back, *Every time.*

Thanks, Maize, Evie sent, and those few minutes of texting became the highlight of Maizee's day. Heck, probably her entire week.

She stood and put together a quick dinner of pork chops and peas, feeling very un-Hawaiian. But she did eat on the back porch while the sun went down, pondering her mother's question.

Will you be joining us for Thanksgiving or Christmas?

Maizee didn't want to go home for the holidays, but the thought of being alone was infinitely worse. Maybe it didn't matter that she didn't like being alone. That didn't mean she wasn't herself when she was with someone. Did it?

She didn't think so. She still got dressed, did her hair, and put on makeup just to sit at her kitchen table and answer emails. She was who she was. She *was* high maintenance with jewelry and makeup and clothing.

So what?

After dinner, she walked Roger and returned home, the quietness in the house almost unnerving. She turned on the Internet radio, navigated a conversation with Hope Sorensen down at Your Tidal Forever, the wedding planning service she'd told her sister Jules about. Since Jules wasn't here on the island, some things had fallen to Maizee, and she ended up scheduling an appointment to go down to the shop on Monday during lunch to look at fabric samples.

When she entered the shop, she was overwhelmed with the sheer bridal nature of it. Lacy curtains and scented pillows on the seating over to the side. A pretty woman sat at a desk, and she jumped to her feet when Maizee walked in.

"Hello." A smile stretched her mouth. "Can I help you?"

"I have a meeting with a woman named Hope? About a dress?" She stretched out her hand for the other woman to shake. "I'm Maizee Phelps. It's for my—"

"Your sister Juliet." The woman nodded. "I'm Riley, and we have the green room ready for you."

"Ooh, the green room," Maizee said with a smile. "Lead on, Riley." She followed the other woman who wore pencil skirts and had every hair in place, with silver hoops swinging from her ears. Maizee thought maybe she could be friends with this woman, and as she stepped through a doorway and into a room that had green paint on the walls, a bright green table in the middle of it, and mint green curtains hanging on the window, she knew instantly that she'd be hiring Your Tidal Forever to plan her wedding. If she ever made it that far in a relationship, that was.

"Here you are," she said. "Ash and Hope will be in soon." Riley flashed a smile and backed out of the room. "Can I get you something to drink?"

"Sure, I'll take some water."

Riley nodded and left completely. She'd been gone maybe two seconds before the door opened again and a petite woman dwarfed with white fabrics entered. Maizee lunged forward to help her, and the woman who introduced herself as Ash Fox, the dress designer, spread out the cloth on the table. It looked even whiter against the green of the table.

A moment later, another dark-haired woman entered and said, "Oh, Ash, you're here. Good. Hello, Maizee."

"You must be Hope." Maizee shook her hand too. "Let me call my sister." She opened her video chat app and pressed the only contact she had in it: Jules. They'd spent the last couple of days getting things set up and practicing.

"Hey," Jules chirped, perfectly put together for this call with her wedding planner. "Hi, Hope. Let me see Ash."

Maizee held the phone so Jules could talk with her people, and then Ash went through the fabrics, showed sketches to Jules, and they talked about what would work with the venue—Jules had decided on the backyard, as long as Hope could transform it into the most beautiful Hawaiian garden anyone had ever seen.

She'd sent pictures to Hope, and the wedding planner had assured her that everything would be beautiful for Jules's big day.

And their mother had been ecstatic. Maizee had learned that her younger sister still listened to her, as she'd been the one to tell Jules, "Look, Mom just wants you to be happy, but she's investing a lot in this. Would it kill you to have the wedding in the backyard? She's been maintaining in for that purpose for twenty years."

Jules had resisted the idea at first, and Maizee hadn't brought it up again. But a couple of weeks later, Maizee had gotten a text from her mother that Jules had agreed o have the wedding in the backyard. Maizee had been as surprised as she'd acted, and she hoped Jules was being nicer to their mother.

The meeting took Maizee's entire lunch hour and then some, but she stayed to the end to make sure Jules could get all of her questions answered. Plus, Maizee didn't want to have to come back here for a while. This place screamed at her that she needed to get married, as if she didn't already know.

And as if she hadn't already been dreaming about walking down the aisle to meet Lawrence, say I do, and kiss him as his wife.

Maizee's anger grew as she drove back to the bank. She wanted to be with Lawrence. So why was she preventing herself from being with him?

At the bank, she sat in the car for an extra moment, thinking about what today's lunch hour would've been like had she been wearing Lawrence's diamond. For one, he would've been there with her. For two, they'd be at lunch right now instead of lamenting the fact that they hadn't eaten yet and didn't have time to eat before getting back to work.

And she was tired of pretending like she wanted to be alone when she didn't.

She thought a lot about how Lawrence had been expanding his horizons, trying to be brave enough to go hiking in unknown trails and out in sea kayaks. He'd calmed her when she was freaking out, and while he'd avoided some things she wished he would've taken on, she wanted to be with him.

So she had to be brave too.

She unbuckled and went inside, bypassing her office and taking the steps up to the second level. To her right, a door said SECURITY in all capital letters, and there was only a couple of other doors. Restrooms from what she could see at the end of the hall, and one more door that had Lawrence's name affixed to the wall outside of it.

The door was open, and she had no idea if he'd be inside the office or not. Her heart beat in her chest, loudly, as if it were an empty drum. But she hadn't come this far for nothing. She stepped over to the door and knocked, saying, "Lawrence?" before peering inside.

His office was empty, as the huge wall of windows and all the light they let in revealed. She marveled at the size of this place—it was easily as large as her entire house. He could section off the end of it and make a bedroom, and with the bathroom right down the hall and how he never cooked, he could live in this office.

Two couches had been arranged in an L, and she didn't dare sit on them because they looked like no one had ever done so before. His desk was covered with papers and folders, but it wasn't in a messy way. His computer screen showed the screen saver, which meant he hadn't been there for a while.

Maizee wandered over to the windows and gazed out of them. The building was only two stories tall, but she could still see across the street, through the treetops, and the slip of blue on the horizon that was the ocean.

No wonder Lawrence spent so much time up here. He had beautiful views, and she knew how much he loved to work, so this place was probably a little slice of heaven for him. The whole room smelled like him, like his musky cologne and fresh cotton scent.

She turned and found a clothing rod holding several suits and an array of ties. Classic Lawrence, and somehow Maizee liked seeing extra clothes there, because it meant he liked to look good too.

His voice came up the stairs, getting closer and closer, and Maizee panicked. Should she rush over to the door so he could see her as soon as he reached the top of the steps? Or take a seat on the couch and pretend to be engrossed in her phone?

"…I don't know, Mom," he said, almost upon her now, and she hadn't even moved from the windows.

She still stood there when he entered his office. He froze, his phone still at his ear. He stared at her and blinked, pure shock on his face.

"I need to call you back," he said. He hung up and lowered his hand to his side.

"Hello," Maizee said, lifting her fingers in a little wave. Foolishness raced through her, and she wound her fingers around themselves. "I just wondered if maybe…I don't know. Maybe you had time to talk?"

"About what?"

He looked dashing in a light gray suit, his hair all swept up, those eyes dark and dreamy. Maizee's stomach quaked, but she didn't want to go home alone tonight.

She opened her mouth to say something, and "I don't

want to go home alone tonight," came out. She sucked in a breath and wanted to pull back in the word *tonight*. But more streamed from her instead. "I miss you. I don't need to be alone. I love you. I don't want to spend the holidays alone. I—"

He held up one hand, and she stopped talking as if he'd pushed mute on her vocal chords. "Let's back up and go one step at a time. I think you started with you miss me?"

Maizee couldn't tell if he was being serious or if he was teasing her. Those dark-as-night eyes sparkled, but the glint in them was hard to decipher.

And she'd come this far. "Yes," she said. "You heard me right."

"And you don't need to be alone." He took a step toward her, obviously in much better control of his faculties than she was.

"I don't," she said, suddenly itching to have his hands cradle her face, touch her skin, hold her close. She knew what she'd said next, and Lawrence had obviously heard her too.

Was he going to make her say it again?

He took another step toward her, his face deadly serious and pure electricity sparking from his eyes.

EIGHTEEN

LAWRENCE'S CHEST squeezed and squeezed, like someone had wound a huge rubber band around him and was twisting it tighter and tighter.

And tighter.

He'd heard what Maizee had said.

I love you.

I don't want to spend the holidays alone.

He loved her too, and he definitely didn't want to spend his holidays alone.

"You have a nice office," she said, and Lawrence saw her slipping into her freaked out mode. "I haven't been here long," she continued, glancing around and then turning back to the windows. "I swear. And I didn't touch anything."

"Maizee," he said, drawing her back to him. "You love me?"

She threw up her arms in exasperation, and her chin wobbled. "Do I have to say it again?"

He nodded, advancing toward her again. "Yes. Yeah, I'm definitely going to need to hear you say that again."

Her eyes turned glassy; her chin came up. "I'm in love with you."

"I love you too," he said quickly, because it seemed like she was going to keep talking. "And I don't want to spend the holidays alone either." He reached up and trailed his fingers through her hair, something he'd been wanting to do for months. "Or my evenings. Or my weekends." He touched his forehead to hers, the time to be the bravest he'd ever needed to in front of him.

"I'm sorry I didn't claim you as my girlfriend to my employees, to the bank, to everyone."

"The case is settled."

"Yes, it is." He put one arm around her waist, glad when she inched closer to him and put both hands on his chest.

"I'm sorry I stayed silent when I should've called you."

"We're both guilty of that."

He supposed she was right. After all, they both had working phones. "I missed you so much," he whispered. "I hate my penthouse. I hate how big this office is. I hate that I can't lay in your hammock and watch the sun set from your backyard."

She wrapped her arms around him too. "You don't like your penthouse?"

"It's too big, and you've never even been there."

"Why is that?" She leaned back and looked at him with those great big blue eyes that had pulled at him since the first moment he'd met her.

He shrugged. "My place...I liked your house better."

She tilted her head slightly but didn't ask another question.

"I'm not perfect," he said, his voice lowering to a near whisper. "I know that. I'm good at some things and bad at others. And I've made some mistakes with you, but I'm going to fix them. I swear. I am."

Maizee tucked herself right back into his chest, and said, "I could say all of those same things."

"So we'll just try harder," he said. "Okay?"

And there was no better word in that moment than, "Okay."

———

Lawrence took off the blue shirt and reached for the gray one. Honestly, he'd never cared what color he wore before, but he also hadn't been expecting to meet Maizee's family quite so soon after they'd gotten back together.

He decided on the gray and tossed the blue one back in his suitcase just as Maizee knocked for the second time. "Larry?" she tried this time.

He shook his head and smiled before stepping over to the door to open it. "Sorry, I was just changing."

She raked her eyes from the top of his head to his feet and back. "This looks great." She reached up and fiddled with the buttons on his collar. "They're going to love you."

"You sound like you're trying to convince yourself."

She blinked at him for a moment and gave a nervous giggle. "It's been a while since I brought someone new home."

"Did Winn come to family dinners a lot?"

"Yes," she said. "But he always wanted to go to his parents' place too, so our visits were always cut short."

"Well, I never see my parents," he said. "So we'll probably see yours a lot." He watched her for a reaction, and she just kept fiddling with his buttons.

"Or we can make our own traditions," she said. "In Getaway Bay. Maybe your mom or dad would come see us there." She looked up at him then, and Lawrence had thought there was no way he could love her more. But in that moment, he did.

"Memories in the penthouse?" he asked.

"If that's what you want," she said. "Can we see the sun set from there?"

"It's on the twentieth floor," he said. "So I think seeing the sunset is a definite possibility."

"Mm. Now remember, Jules will not want to be upstaged. We just nod and smile at her."

"Nod and smile," he said. "I can do that."

"And Evie is bringing Tommy too, and that's a very big deal for her," Maizee said, repeating the things she'd been telling him for a week.

"But we like Tommy," Lawrence said.

"Yes," Maizee said. "You'll see."

"I've met people before," Lawrence said.

"You said you've not met a woman's family before."

"No, but I've met people. Believe it or not, I'm quite good at small talk." He smiled gently at her. "There is something I wanted to talk to you about."

"Oh?" She stepped out of his arms and into the hall outside his hotel room.

"Yeah." He swallowed, checked to make sure he had his room key, and took her hand in his. "It's about marriage."

She stopped walking as if her feet had grown roots. "What?"

Heat shot to Lawrence's face. "Well, I just thought—"

"You are not asking me to marry you this weekend." She started shaking her head so violently, her hair swung back and forth, fanning out. "Nope. Not happening."

"Why not?" Lawrence may have bought a ring already. They'd been back together for almost three weeks. And he'd packed it and brought it with him.

"This is the totally wrong time," she said. "My sister is getting married and my other one is in the first serious relationship she's been excited about in a year." She gave her head one final shake. "No." She gave him a very serious stare over the top of the sedan he'd rented to get them around the island.

"All right," he said, feeling completely out of his element. "When would be a good time?"

She ducked her head and tucked her hair, one of his favorite gestures. "Oh, surprise me."

"Just not this weekend."

"Not this weekend." She opened her door and slid into the car, leaving him little choice but to do the same. Lawrence followed her directions around the twisty roads, finally pulling into a modest home surrounded by tons of trees.

He had no idea how to surprise a woman like Maizee,

but at least he had something new to obsess about now. Too bad it couldn't happen right now, as the front door of the house opened before he could even unbuckle.

Two women spilled out, obviously Maizee's sisters, what with the blonde hair and the blue eyes and the smiles as wide as the Mississippi. They flew down the steps as Maizee said, "Jules is in front," and got out of the car.

They'd slowed to a walk by the time Lawrence met her at the front of the car and took her hand in his. "Ready?" she said, but he didn't have time to answer before her sisters stood only a few feet away.

"Hello," Jules said, her hair a darker shade of blonde than Maizee, and infinitely lighter than the third sister— Evie.

Jules batted her clearly false eyelashes at Lawrence, and Maizee's hand in his tightened. "This is Juliet," Maizee said. "She's engaged to Johnny. Remember I told you about Johnny?"

"Right," Lawrence said, wanting to do everything to make Maizee's life easier, including this Thanksgiving trip to see her family. "Johnny. He owns the body shop." He gave Jules his widest, most political smile, the one he gave the photographers when he was getting headshots taken.

"Yes," Maizee said, almost robotically. "And Evelyn. She brought Tommy for dinner too."

"Of course." He shook Evie's hand, and she seemed sane. All three of the Phelps sisters were remarkably well put together, right down to the accessories. "Tommy's the paramedic, right?"

Evie grinned and nodded. "That's right. And he's

currently out back with Dad—alone." She gave Maizee a pointed look.

"She can't figure out how to get out there without seeming like she wants to save him." Jules giggled.

"Is Johnny here?" Maizee asked, taking a step toward the front door. The sisters went too, Jules explaining how Johnny was trying to make a pumpkin pie for their feast in a few hours and it was still in the oven.

Lawrence didn't believe her for a second, but no one questioned her. They climbed the steps, still chattering, and Lawrence waited to go last. His nerves seemed to be firing and skipping, bumping around underneath his skin. Her father was out in the yard, so he'd only have to meet her mother right now.

The older blonde woman stood in the kitchen, wearing an Anne of Green Gables apron and stirring something on the stove with vigor.

"Hey, Mom," Maizee said, and her mother glanced up.

She did not stop stirring, but said, "Evie, come finish this."

Evie complied, and Maizee's mother turned toward them, wiped her hands on her apron and then fixed her hair before coming over to meet Lawrence.

"Hello," he said, glancing real quick at Maizee, his mind blanking as to her mother's name.

In the next moment, she latched onto him and said, "Welcome to our home." She kissed one cheek and then the other and stepped back, her face happy and beaming. The whole house smelled like roasted turkey and something sweet, and

Lawrence really hoped there would be plantains and poi for dinner.

"Thank you for having me," Lawrence said, his voice a bit on the thick side. It felt…nice to have a mother's touch, to be hugged like she knew him and loved him. She moved over to Maizee, hugged her, and then turned back to the kitchen.

"Jules, we need punch made and those plantains peeled."

"I hate peeling plantains."

"You eat more of them than anyone," Maizee said, quickly stepping back over to Lawrence. "Her name is Linnie. Dad is Lorenzo."

"Incoming," Evie said as she passed, a quick nod toward the windows at the back of the house. "Dad's on his way in."

Lorenzo, Lorenzo, Lorenzo, Lawrence recited to himself, saying it and smiling and shaking the man's hand once they were introduced. He met Tommy too, and the guy seemed nice enough. He held Evie's hand, and they seemed to have a whole conversation just by looking at each other.

Lawrence liked that, liked that Maizee had somehow known he'd blanked on her mother's name.

"So, Lawrence," Lorenzo said. "What do you like to do?"

He looked at Maizee, trying to find a couple of one-word answers he could give. She gazed steadily back at him, those blue eyes sparkling like sapphires.

"I'm kind of an indoor person," he said. "But I do like sailing and hiking."

Lorenzo smiled, and Lawrence was glad he could give the right answer. The couple of hours before dinner passed quickly, with Johnny showing up a mere five minutes before the meal began. He carried a store-bought pumpkin pie and gave Jules a quick kiss on the cheek before launching into a story about how everything he'd tried with the homemade pumpkin pie had ended in disaster.

Then he tucked himself in at the table without even noticing Lawrence was there. When he finally looked up and caught Lawrence's eye, he nearly choked. "I know you," he said, reaching for a napkin.

"This is Maizee's boyfriend," Linnie said. "Lawrence Gladstone."

Johnny wiped his mouth, his eyes wide, but Lawrence couldn't tell if he was nervous or awed. "Yeah, my loan on the body shop is from Gladstone Financial. I get a newsletter every month with your picture in it."

"Ah, yes." Lawrence smiled and speared another forkful of the most delicious fried plantains he'd ever had the pleasure of eating. He cut a quick look at Maizee. "Those newsletters are quite infamous."

She giggled but he just kept his smile in place until Jules moved the conversation to her wedding.

NINETEEN

"HE HASN'T ASKED YOU YET?" Maizee wanted to yank the phone around in a full circle, which would make Jules dizzy. At least then she'd shut up.

"These are the centerpieces," she said, holding the phone as still as she could as she moved down the table. "Hope said you have five choices for the package you chose."

"We don't need centerpieces," Jules said. "I've told her that a million times." She made a scoffing noise of disgust. "Honestly, the wedding is in six months. I could get a new planner, right?"

"No way." Maizee turned the phone back so she could see her sister's face. "Jules, this place is amazing. All the people here are *amazing*. There's no way you can get better than this." She tried to convey the urgency of her words by giving them a few seconds of silence.

"All the flowers are locally sourced. She probably just forgot."

"We're using the garden flowers for centerpieces."

"Oh, that's right," Hope said, clicking the last few steps toward them. "But you still need corsages, right?" She pressed her face in close to Maizee's so Jules could see them both.

"Yes," Jules said.

"Let's keep moving down then," Hope said, and she took over the rest of the meeting, thankfully. Once the call with Jules was disconnected, she said, "So, when are you booking your tidal forever?"

Over the few months Maizee had been coming to the shop to help her sister, she'd gotten to know a few of the women there, Hope especially. "He hasn't asked yet," she said for what felt like the millionth time. "Honestly, when I told him not to ask that weekend, I assumed he'd do it the next day." She blew out her breath and adjusted a bangle on her wrist. "But he hasn't even brought it up again."

"Is there anything special coming up?" Hope asked.

"You mean, besides Valentine's Day?" They'd spent Christmas together in his penthouse, decorating a huge tree and making hot chocolate. Snuggling by the fake fire. Talking about their lives and if they wanted children, dogs, a lot of land, a white picket fence. All of it.

"Maybe he's waiting for that."

"I don't want to get engaged on Valentine's Day." Maizee made a face. "Surely he won't wait that long." She glanced at Hope, desperate for confirmation. "Will he?"

"I don't know him all that well." Hope gave her a reassuring smile. "But what about your birthday? Or his? Maybe he's waiting for something special."

Lawrence was a waiter, that was for sure. "Maybe I just need to tell him I'm ready," Maizee mused. The scent of garlic bread met her nose, and she turned toward the front office.

"Feeding everyone today?" she asked.

"A supplier lunch," Hope confirmed. "That's why I was late. Do you want to stay?"

Maizee's stomach grumbled, but she shook her head. "No, but thanks." She gave Hope a quick squeeze and headed for the exit. She'd call Lawrence and ask him to lunch—where she'd bring up the topic of marriage.

By the time she'd called Lawrence's phone four times without getting him to answer, she knew something was wrong. He hadn't told her he'd be away from his phone, and she wondered if he'd gone out hiking. Maybe to the beach. He said he'd been visiting it a lot more lately, because it wasn't high tourist season and the sand didn't bother him so much now that he'd learned about the showers up by the buildings that lined the road. Then he could rinse off his feet before stuffing them back into his shiny leather shoes.

Maizee had laughed for a long time over that. She'd told him that most people wore flip flops to the beach, and swim trunks, and hey, she'd really like to see him without a shirt on.

But he took off his tie and loosened his collar, removed his shoes and socks, and dug in.

She tried to call him again, with the same result—voice mail.

At that point, her worry lifted, and she left a message, "Lawrence, I've called five times. Are you okay? Can you at least text to let me know you're alive and I don't need to call the police?"

She stared out the windshield, wondering if she should just go to the beach and walk the sand until she found him. She hung up and sighed, her stomach still grumbling about the lack of food inside it.

Her phone buzzed, and she couldn't look at it fast enough. But it wasn't Lawrence. Instead, Tawny's name sat on the screen. *Are you coming to class today?*

The yoga classes were held a little later in the day during the winter months, especially on the weekends, and she could get in a workout and then grab lunch right on the beach. She wasn't exactly dressed for yoga, but at least she wasn't wearing a skirt.

Sure, I'll be there in a minute.

Maizee put the car in drive and pulled out of the lot. Nothing was very far in Getaway Bay, though it did take several minutes to drive up and around the bay and along the main drag that led to Getaway Bay from East Bay.

She parked across the street, because there were so many cars on the beach side, which she found very odd. Maybe there were a lot of tourists here at the end of January, or a big convention at the hotel. Something, because there were so many people on the beach already, Maizee couldn't even see the yoga class.

Glancing around, she locked her car and shouldered her purse. There was definitely something going on. Something big. Maybe Sweet Breeze had hosted a wedding, as she could see streamers waving as the breeze picked up.

Men in suits stood on the beachwalk as she went past, all

of them watching her. She'd been a head-turner in her life once, but their undivided attention was a bit odd.

And then she recognized one of them. She paused, almost stumbling though she wore flats. She turned back and looked at the impeccably dressed man. "Do I know you?" He had dark hair and blue eyes and exuded power from those broad shoulders. He was so much like Lawrence, and she realized she was staring at his friends.

"Have you seen Lawrence?" she asked next, when none of the six men standing there had said a word.

The one she recognized—she was almost sure he owned the hotel they were loitering outside of—nodded down toward the beach. "He's out there somewhere."

"Does he have his phone?"

"Does Lawrence go anywhere without his phone?" The man chuckled and looked at his friends. One shook his head, and he looked a bit familiar too. Maybe she'd seen him in one of her financial magazines.

But he didn't even wear a suit, but that pair of board shorts and faded T-shirt she wished Lawrence would put on when he went to the beach. He grinned at her and pointed toward the beach. "I just saw him out there. Looked like he was going to take the yoga class."

Maizee spun, her heart suddenly hammering. But she couldn't see anything. "Am I supposed to go down there?"

"If you want to take the yoga class," one of the men said behind her.

She left without saying anything else, her feet suddenly bent on making it to the yoga class as quickly as possible. There were people *everywhere*, and she pushed through the crowd, hoping she was going in the right direction to get to beach yoga.

As she moved closer, she heard, "…that's it. All the way down," in Tawny's soothing voice over a speaker. "Feel the energy from the ground. Let it flow through you."

Maizee saw the streamers flowing, and if she could just get past a few more people, she'd be in the square where the class was held. She finally burst onto the scene—but there was no one there.

No class.

No Tawny.

"Oh," her voice said through the speaker. "Our guest of honor has arrived."

Maizee looked around, trying to find her friend. Or anyone else who might even be a little bit familiar. The space where the yoga class was usually held was shaded by a huge pergola, obviously hand built. White, blue, and pink streamers waved lazily in the wind, and the scent of roses floated on the air.

"What—?"

Lawrence appeared on the other side of the square, so close and yet impossibly far away. He wore slacks and a light blue dress shirt, open at the throat. Maizee's breath hitched in her chest. He wasn't here to do yoga.

And she wasn't either.

Tawny stepped beside him and reached up to clip the mic to his collar. After several seconds of silence, she practically shoved him out into the open sand. Lawrence stumbled, but at least he wasn't wearing his thousand-dollar shoes.

Instead, he was barefoot and holding one hand behind his back.

Maizee started across the sand toward him, noting that the noise level had dropped considerably. "Lawrence," she said, glad he'd begun walking too. "What's going on?"

People stepped out from the crowd, making Maizee stall before she reached Lawrence. She recognized these faces— Kara from Roasted, Polly and Willie from work, Tawny and Hope and Riley.

They each held red roses, and Maizee's hand went to her mouth. "Oh my…."

Lawrence reached her then, one hand cradling her elbow. "Hey, Maizee." The smile that crossed his face could certainly achieve world peace. "I got your message, but then I heard you were on your way over here."

"What's going on?" she whispered, already knowing but wanting him to say it.

"I'm in love with you," he said, running one hand through her hair. His eyes burned with an intensity she'd never seen. He dropped to both knees in front of her, bringing that hidden hand in front of him. "I had this big speech all prepared." He gave a nervous chuckle, but Maizee honestly couldn't breathe.

"But I've sort of forgotten it." Lawrence glanced up as Tawny handed him her rose. One by one, the other people Maizee had gotten to know over the past few months gave Lawrence their flowers too.

In a matter of a minute, he held a dozen roses and a diamond ring in his hands. He gazed up at her. "I love you so much. Will you marry me?"

Tears sprang to her eyes, and her whole face felt like it would split with the smile she couldn't contain. She nodded, her tears splashing her face. "Yes." Her voice sounded like she hadn't used it in years.

"Yeah?"

"Yes," she said again, louder.

He slid the ring on her finger, his hands warm and wonderful against hers. She gazed at it, took the roses from him, and melted right into his arms. He kissed her, and she didn't even care there was a huge group of people watching. They cheered and music started, and then they were surrounded by all the people that cared about them most.

TWENTY

LAWRENCE ENTERED Fisher's penthouse a few minutes after their Nine-0 meeting was supposed to start. Nothing was official, and their meetings didn't have a schedule. But every eye was still drawn to him, and he smiled as he moved over to the counter and picked up two cans of Dr. Pepper.

"Hey, Fish," he said to the man standing there. "How's the baby?"

"Doing so great." Fisher grinned and lifted his water bottle to his lips. "What about you? Getting married tomorrow." He glanced at Lawrence, who nodded.

"Yeah. Ready." Lawrence was more than ready. Beyond ready. It had been a great ten months with Maizee as his fiancée, but it had been *ten months*. He was dying to start his life with her as his wife, but she'd needed time to plan every detail. And if there was one thing he knew about Maizee, it was that she was crazy about details.

While her sister had been married in their parent's back-yard, Maizee had chosen to stay here in Getaway Bay and have a beach wedding right here at Sweet Breeze. She'd hired Your Tidal Forever to plan her wedding, and Lawrence had gone to tastings for cake, meetings to pick out center-pieces, and appointments to go over invitations.

The only thing he hadn't done was help Maizee with her dress. She said she didn't want him to see her in it until she was walking down the aisle, and he'd agreed.

"And you're giving up the penthouse," Fisher said.

"Yeah," Lawrence said. "She has a great backyard, and it's…." He wasn't sure what it was about her place that he liked so much. Maybe just that she was there. "I'll miss Linus and Isabella," he said, changing the subject. "But I invested in the Orcas, and we got box seats together, so I'll still get to see them." The team hadn't had a great first season, but Linus was convinced they just needed a few years to get established. They'd just hired an ex-quarterback as their new offensive coach, and Linus was overly excited about having McCoy Armstrong on the staff.

"Well, we'll all be there," Fisher said. "Stacey says Jonah is fine to be around people now."

"You sure?" Lawrence asked. "I mean, I want Stacey there, but not if the baby is sick. We understand."

"She says it's okay," Fisher said. "So we'll be there." He grinned at Lawrence and said, "I need to go talk to Marshall for a sec. See you tomorrow."

"See you." Lawrence's stomach swooped. Tomorrow. He was finally getting married *tomorrow*.

Tomorrow came quickly in a string of days that had seemed to take forever to pass. He adjusted his cufflinks and looked in the mirror. Behind him, his father did the same thing, fixing all the pieces of his suit and his shirt before joining Lawrence.

"Thanks for having me," he said for probably the tenth time that day.

Instant annoyance sprang through Lawrence, but he kept his voice even when he said, "Of course." He didn't need to be thanked for inviting his own family to his wedding. He was a bit surprised they'd all made the journey across the ocean, but he'd been nothing but grateful and helpful, putting them all up in Sweet Breeze and going back and forth to the airport to pick them all up.

His mother and sisters had been in town for a few days, and he'd only left them alone for an hour to attend his Nine-0 Club meeting the previous day. Maizee had taken them to lunch, and they were with her in the bride's room.

Sudden nerves hit him, and he couldn't wait to get out on the beach.

"I wasn't sure you'd ever get married," his dad said, and Lawrence suppressed a sigh.

"Yeah, well, Gladstone Financial takes a lot time and energy." He met his dad's eyes in the mirror for a brief moment. He didn't need to justify anything to his father, and what good would it do to tell him that it was partially his fault Lawrence had believed a marriage could never work?

After all, the man had been married four times. So Lawrence smiled and said, "It's probably time," before turning and walking over to the door. He cracked it, having been given very specific instructions from a woman named Charlotte that he was not to exit before she gave him the signal.

The hallway outside was empty, and he closed the door again. From the window, he could see the set-up on the beach, and the ceremony would take place under the same pergola where he'd proposed.

Maizee had changed the pink and blue streamers out for gold and navy blue, with a hint of hunter green. She wanted it to echo Christmas without screaming with red and green. Chairs had been set up and extra tents erected to cover them.

People moved around down there, probably guests taking their seats. He wished he could get the window open so he could hear the ocean, but he supposed the wedding music would drown out the waves.

Someone knocked on the door, startling him away from the paradise before him. He answered the door to find Charlotte standing there. "Ready, Mister Gladstone?"

"Yes, ma'am."

She gave him a smile and said, "You can go on down. All the way to the altar, like we discussed. You're using the main bank of elevators. Please don't deviate from that, okay?"

"All right," he said, twisting to call over his shoulder, "Come on, Dad."

Charlotte leaned closer and said in a whisper, "His seat is on the very end of the second row, on the right."

"Thank you," Lawrence said, and she left before his dad could cross the room to him. "Let's go, Dad." They made their way down the hall and onto the appointed elevator. Lawrence didn't wear shoes, which he was glad for when he stepped onto the sand. He directed his father to the correct seat, which was far enough from his mother to appease everyone.

He crossed over to the other corner of the crowd, where his mother sat with both of his sisters, their husbands, and all of his nieces and nephews. "Hey, guys." He gathered all the kids into a group hug amidst giggles. "You ready for this boring party?"

"It's not boring," Lois said, patting the chair for her son to come sit back down. "This is the best wedding we've been to, right Mom?"

"The food is so good here," his mother said, and Lawrence leaned down and kissed her forehead.

"I'm so glad you guys came."

"You'll be here for a few more days, right?" Lawrence hadn't really paid too much attention to their plans post-wedding, as he and Maizee were traveling over the next couple of weeks for their honeymoon. She'd planned a trip to Europe, somewhere she'd always wanted to visit.

"Yes, until Wednesday," his other sister, Sally, said. "Thanks for everything, Larry."

He gave her a hug too and figured his time until he was supposed to be stationed at the altar was up. So he straightened his tie and took his position at the front of the crowd. His heart beat and beat and beat with every minute that passed.

Why wasn't Maizee coming? Had something happened?

What if she didn't show up?

Lawrence pushed the doubts away. Maizee loved him. She'd be here.

He scanned the crowd, glad when the pastor arrived with a big smile and a "Are you ready?"

Lawrence nodded and jerked his attention to the back of the chairs that had been set up when the frilly music filtering through the overhead speakers quieted and then changed to the wedding march.

Fisher linked arms with Stacey, and both of them grinned like fools as they took step by slowly painful step down the aisle. All of Lawrence's friends were in the wedding party, as were the few Maizee had made since she'd been on the island.

It seemed to take forever for them to all move down the aisle so he could see Maizee. Everything inside him froze at the sight of her in that gorgeous, flowing, head-to-toe lace dress. She wore a radiant smile and her hair all pinned up on the top of her head. She carried a bouquet of the most gorgeous pink flowers he'd ever seen, and Lawrence felt like he was the luckiest man in the world.

She arrived in front of him, and he received her into his arms. "Hey, my beautiful fiancée."

"Almost wife," she whispered with an anxious giggle.

"Nervous?" he asked.

She shook her head and smiled before turning to face the pastor. The ceremony began, and Lawrence tried really hard to pay attention. But the soft smell of her perfume infusing the air around him, and the feel of her tucked against his side made listening very difficult.

He did hear her when she said, "I do," and he knew enough to say the same thing when it was his turn.

And he definitely heard the pastor when he said, "I now pronounce you husband and wife. You may kiss your bride."

Lawrence looked at Maizee, giddiness trampling through him as she gazed back at him with fire and electricity in her expression. He held her tight and kissed her, kissed her, kissed her, the crowd behind them cheering like they'd just won the billion-dollar lottery.

Lawrence definitely felt like he had, and he whispered, "I love you, Maizee," one more time before kissing her again.

———

Read on for a sneak peek of the first chapter of **GETAWAY BAY SINGLES**, the last book in the Getaway Bay Resort series.

SNEAK PEEK! GETAWAY BAY SINGLES CHAPTER ONE

KATHERINE HARRISON SIGHED as she sat down, her bowl of chicken noodle soup rotating in the microwave behind her. The break room at Clean Sweep needed a thorough cleaning, ironic considering this was a maid service.

The biggest, best maid service on the island of Getaway Bay. With a dirty break room. As the owner of the company, she should clean it, but she couldn't get up the energy to do much more than swipe right on her phone as she looked at her dating app.

Getaway Bay Singles promised to be the "directional compass in your dating life" much like a GPS was to help someone get around the island. GBS boasted high percentages of singles getting together and staying together right here on the island, and Katie had decided to join the service because she was tired of managing the seventeen people at Clean Sweep and then going home to take care of her ten-year-old daughter.

Heather was awesome, and Katie didn't mind being a mother or a business owner. She was just lonely. So lonely.

And GBS helped with that, so she was glad she'd joined though she hadn't made much of a love connection yet. She tapped and swiped through the app, reading quick sentence like *AndrewB and JoanS went to Spam Hut*, and *MikeT and TerriL enjoyed an island tour*.

GBS helped with restaurants, date ideas, and more. She'd filled out all of her favorites the first night she'd downloaded the app, staying up well past her bedtime to do so. But if she ever were to meet a man in real life from the app, she felt certain they'd have an excellent meal at a restaurant they both liked. The app would not lead them astray, that much Katie knew.

She'd been chatting with a man named TeddyF for several days, and a message from him popped up on her screen. *Surviving the week?*

Sort of, she typed back to him, a smile brightening her face and her day. *Sooo busy this week.*

Cleaning, right? his next message said.

Right. Katie had told him about herself, as many as the surface things as she felt comfortable with. Favorite movie, favorite food, what she liked to do in her spare time. The thought of spare time was actually laughable, but she wasn't laughing.

She had one more thing to tell him before she'd be comfortable getting together with him, and she set her phone down as she thought through their few weeks of conversation. She liked him. He was witty and smart. Thoughtful and inquisitive. He'd been kind, and while his profile picture was a cartoon rendition of him, she thought he was probably attractive, in an older, closer-to-fifty silver fox kind of way.

Because Katie had faced it—she wasn't exactly a spring chicken at age forty-six.

TeddyF liked Chinese food, and warm island rain, and the view from the highest point in Getaway Bay. He worked in the technology sector as an app developer. He'd only been on the island for thirteen months, and he claimed he hadn't had a serious relationship in years and years.

One or two dates is all, he'd told her. *And then the spark is gone.*

When she'd asked him if he was looking for serious, he'd given her one word: *Yes.*

And while Katie had had serious twice now, she had to admit she didn't want to move into her fifties and then sixties by herself.

I have something to tell you, she typed, her fingers moving in a methodical and slow way. *And you can take your time responding. Think about it. All of that.*

Oh, boy, he said. *All right. Go ahead.*

I have a ten-year-old daughter named Heather. Katie stared at the words. She'd only told three men on GBS about Heather, and all three of them had cooled considerably afterward. But honestly, did they think they were courting a forty-six-year-old woman without any ties or responsibilities?

TeddyF was forty-nine, at least according to his profile. She'd learned that most men didn't lie on GBS. There wasn't really a point, as it was an app for singles in a very limited location, not across-the-ocean correspondence.

Am I meant to guess the thing you need to tell me? ;)

Katie startled at the ding and resulting vibration in her hands from his message. A light laugh tickled her vocal chords, and she tapped on the arrow to send her sentence through the magic of the WiFi to TeddyF's phone.

Then she flipped her phone over and pushed her chair back. She realized in that moment and with that motion that she didn't want TeddyF to cool considerably after he found out about Heather. She didn't want that at all, and if he asked to meet her, she'd say yes.

"You should ask him," she said aloud just as Lacey entered the break room.

"What?" She pulled open the fridge and pulled out a can of Diet Coke—her lunch.

"Just talking to myself again," Katie said as her phone chimed once, twice, three times.

"Ooh, someone's popular." Lace sat down beside Katie and grinned. "Is that GBS?"

"How did you know?"

"That notification sound is unique."

"Are you using the app?"

"Who doesn't?" Lace shrugged and took a swig of her soda. "So, who's the guy? Are you meeting him?"

"Thinking about it," Katie said, telling her office manager the truth. If there was someone who cared about Clean Sweep as much as Katie, it was Lacey Moon, and she'd been with Katie since the beginning.

She'd also been as unlucky in love, and Katie said, "Have you ever met up with someone on GBS?"

"Yeah, a couple of times." She tossed her dark ponytail

over her shoulder. "The app is pretty amazing and matching up what the two of you like and suggesting the type of date you're likely to enjoy."

"That's what I've heard." Katie's phone *bllliing*ed again, but she still didn't dare pick it up.

"You want me to see what he's saying?"

Katie covered her phone with her hand. "No…." She looked at Lace, a flicker of fear rumbling through her. "I just told him about Heather."

"Oh."

Yeah, that one word said it all, and Katie nodded, her palm still flat against the plastic case of her phone. She drew in a deep breath and said, "Here I go."

Ten years old, Teddy had said. *That's great. My youngest nephew is ten. Great age.*

I like kids, if that's what you're wondering.

And then, his last message was *Did I lose you?*

She looked up at Lace. "He said he likes kids." She wasn't sure why, but her voice held a measure of awe. "What should I do?"

"Ask him out." Lace grinned and finished her can of pop.

"Really? Just like that."

"Just. Like. That." She really hit that last T, and Katie felt the vibrations of it down inside her stomach. Which may not be as flat as it once had been. Maybe she could get together with TeddyF in a couple of weeks, after she'd had a chance to hit it hard on the treadmill, really get that ten pounds off she'd been slowly putting on since moving to paradise and eating more fresh fruit smoothies than was humanly sane.

After all, fruit had calories too. As did the coconut milk

and sugar added to the smoothies that made them so delicious.

"Okay," she said, letting her fingers fly over the screen. "I'm going to do it."

Want to get together sometime? She read the sentence aloud to Lace and waited for the thirty-something to give her approval. When she nodded, Katie hit send.

Absolutely, Teddy said almost instantly. *What are you doing tonight?*

"Tonight?" The disbelief in Katie's voice felt like a lead weight in her lungs. "He wants to get together tonight."

"Great," Lace said, snatching the phone from Katie's fingers. "You're free, right?"

"I need someone to watch Heather."

Lace gave her a semi-disgusted look. "Duh. I'll do it. It's Friday night. You should go out with this…TeddyF. Oh, he's hot."

"His profile picture is a cartoon."

"Yeah, and he's gorgeous, even as an animated head." Lace's thumbs tippity-tapped, and she grinned as she hit send and handed the phone back.

Katie almost didn't dare to look at it. "What did you say?"

"Read it."

Katie rolled her eyes and said, "Doing nothing tonight. Let me see if I can get a sitter." She glanced at Lace. "I'm tired."

"And you're never going to meet the man of your dreams if you take a nap every Friday night."

"It's not every Friday night," Katie grumbled as her phone blinged at her.

I hope you can. I'd love to meet you.

A warmth started in her stomach and radiated outward to all of her limbs. She could make him wait ten minutes before saying she'd found someone to babysit. So she did.

———

Katie sat at an outside table, her heeled foot tapping while she waited. She wasn't being impatient—Teddy wasn't late yet. No, it was nervous energy that had her heel clicking against the stones with the rhythm of a metronome.

Heather hadn't had any homework, not that Katie made her do it on Friday nights. But there'd been absolutely no reason why she couldn't go on this date, and while she didn't really want to cancel, the anxiety over the unknown had her wishing she'd put on a wig and a giant pair of sunglasses before coming to the bistro.

She fingered the ends of her hair, which she'd actually let down out of its customary ponytail, the curl it held naturally quite nice when she wasn't trying to keep it out of the toilet. She'd let Lace switch out the black cardigan for a bright red one, but with the blue and white dress, she felt more like the American flag than a woman ever should.

Every man who walked by sent her heartbeat into a tizzy, but none of them veered into Bora Bora's. Seven o'clock came and then went, and still Teddy hadn't shown up.

The three minutes she waited felt like three years, and

then someone said, "Katie?" in a deep, luxurious voice that reminded her of melted chocolate and marshmallows.

It also sounded very much like… "Theo?" She turned, sure she would not come face-to-face with her ex-husband.

That couldn't happen.

But she stared right into the blazing blue eyes of Theodore Fleming himself. Very much an older version of the man she'd married twenty-five years ago. She blinked, wanting to rub her eyes with her fists.

"Theo?" she said again, half-hopeful that he wouldn't remember her. Which was the most foolish thing she'd ever thought. Of course he's remember her. They'd shared a house and a bed and a life together for five years.

His eyes widened, and he fell back a step. "Katherine?"

She had enough time to take in the gorgeous quality of his silver hair, still with some of that dark brown in there. My, he'd aged very well. Very well, indeed. Those eyes hadn't changed, nor had the fact that he kept his face absolutely clean-shaven.

He wore a black pair of slacks that looked like they'd cost as much as her mortgage, and a cornflower blue polo that accentuated his chest and upper arms. He certainly hadn't put on ten pounds in the past few years, and Katie wanted to flee very, very badly.

"I can't believe you're going by Teddy now," she said with a hint of acid in her voice. He'd never used that nickname in all the years she'd known him. But of course, one of the reasons they'd gotten divorced was because she hadn't known him at all.

"Just on GBS," he said easily, like seeing her after two

decades hadn't affected him at all. Had he ever thought about her? Did he even miss her after she'd declared him having an affair with his obsession to start his own business and walked out?

"It gives me a certain sense of…anonymity." He flashed a smile that definitely held some nerves, and Katie was glad for that. "You never went by Katie."

"Well, I do now," she said, remembering her early twenties when Katherine carried more dignity, and Katie was for little girls.

He pulled out the chair like he would sit and stay. Horror snaked through her. "Mind if I sit?"

"I'm surprised you want to."

He did and gazed at her, an unreadable expression on that handsome face. She'd give Theo that. He'd always been charming and handsome. She'd never doubted him, or the fact that he'd own and operate a very successful business one day. She just didn't want to come second or third or sometimes last to his whims, ideas, dreams, and career.

"So," he said. "Where did the Harrison come from?"

———

Ooh, Katie and Theo used to be married! Read **GETAWAY BAY SINGLES** today!

Aloha Hideaway Inn (Book 1): Can Stacey and the Aloha Hideaway Inn survive strange summer weather, the arrival of the new resort, *and* the start of a special relationship?

Getaway Bay (Book 2): Can Esther deal with dozens of business tasks, unhappy tourists, *and* the twists and turns in her new relationship?

Women's Beach Club (Book 3): With the help of her friends in the Beach Club, can Tawny solve the mystery, stay safe, and keep her man?

Straw and Diamonds (Book 4): Can Sasha maintain her sanity amidst their busy schedules, her issues with men like Jasper, and her desires to take her business to the next level?

The Billionaire Club (Book 5): Can Lexie keep her business affairs in the shadows while she brings her relationship out of them? Or will she have to confess everything to her new friends...and Jason?

Sweet Breeze Resort (Book 6): Can Gina manage her business across the sea and finish the remodel at Sweet Breeze, all while developing a meaningful relationship with Owen and his sons?

Rainforest Retreat (Book 7): As their paths continue to cross and Lawrence and Maizee spend more and more time together, will he find in her a retreat from all the family pressure? Can Maizee manage her relationship with her boss, or will she once again put her heart—and her job—on the line?

Getaway Bay Singles (Book 8): Can Katie bring him into her life, her daughter's life, and manage her business while he manages the app? Or will everything fall apart for a second time?

Turn the page to view series starters from three of my other series!

BOOKS IN THE STRANDED IN GETAWAY BAY® ROMANCE SERIES

Meet the McLaughlin Sisters in Getaway Bay as they encounter disaster after disaster...including the men they get stranded with. From ex-boyfriends to cowboys to football stars, these sisters can bring any man to his knees when the cards are stacked against them.

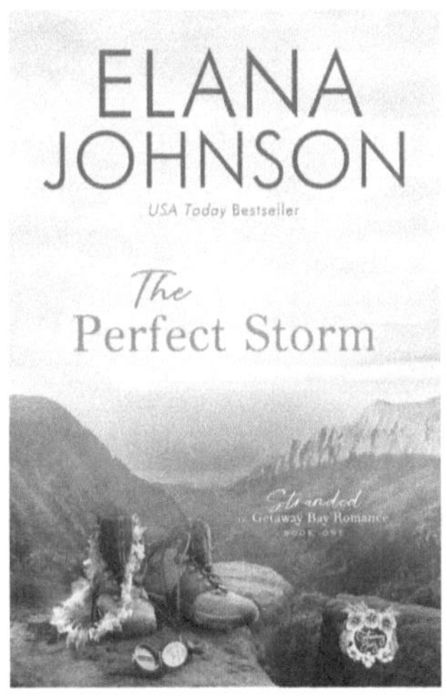

The Perfect Storm (Book 1): A freak storm has her sliding down the mountain...right into the arms of her ex. As Eden and Holden spend time out in the wilds of Hawaii trying to survive, their old flame is rekindled. But with secrets and old feelings in the way, will Holden be able to take all the broken pieces of his life and put them back together in a way that makes sense? Or will he lose his heart and the reputation of his company because of a single landslide?

BOOKS IN THE GETAWAY BAY® ROMANCE SERIES

Escape to Getaway Bay and meet your new best friends as these women navigate their careers, their love lives, and their own dreams and desires. Each heartwarming love story shows the power of women in their own lives and the lives of their friends.

The Island House (Book 1): Charlotte Madsen's whole world came crashing down six months ago with the words, "I met someone else."

Can Charlotte navigate the healing process to find love again?

BOOKS IN THE HILTON HEAD ROMANCE SERIES

Visit the South Carolina Lowcountry and picturesque Hilton Head Island in this sweet women's fiction romance series by USA Today bestselling author, Elana Johnson.

The Love List (Hilton Head Romance, Book 1): Bea turns to her lists when things get confusing and her love list morphs once again... Can she add *fall in love at age 45* to the list and check it off?

ABOUT ELANA

Elana Johnson is the USA Today bestselling and Kindle All-Star author of dozens of clean and wholesome contemporary romance novels. She lives in Utah, where she mothers two fur babies, works with her husband full-time, and eats a lot of veggies while writing. Find her on her website at authorelanajohnson.com

www.ingramcontent.com/pod-product-compliance
Lightning Source LLC
Chambersburg PA
CBHW050313110726
47899CB00007B/2224